open file

PETER CORRIS is known as the 'godfather' of Australian crime fiction through his Cliff Hardy detective stories. He has written in many other areas, including a co-authored autobiography of the late Professor Fred Hollows, a history of boxing in Australia, spy novels, historical novels and a collection of short stories about golf (see www.petercorris.net). He is married to writer Jean Bedford and lives in Sydney. They have three daughters.

PETER CORRIS

open file

A CLIFF HARDY NOVEL

For help in preparation of this book I am grateful to Ruth Corris and Jean Bedford. Beverley Kingston's *A History of New South Wales* (2006) helped to provide period facts and texture.

First published in 2008

Allen & Unwin
83 Alexander Street
Crows Nest NSW 2065
Australia
Phone: (61 2) 8425 0100
Fax: (61 2) 9906 2218
Email: info@allenandunwin.com
Web: www.allenandunwin.com

National Library of Australia
Cataloguing-in-Publication entry:

Corris, Peter, 1942– .

Open file / author, Peter Corris.
Crows Nest, N.S.W. : Allen & Unwin, 2008.
ISBN: 978 1 74175 417 9 (pbk.).

A823.3

Set in 12/14 pt Adobe Garamond by Midland Typesetters, Australia
Printed in Australia by McPherson's Printing Group

10 9 8 7 6 5 4 3 2 1

For Ruth, Michelle and Heath.

part one

Prologue

My Private Enquiry Agent licence was cancelled, my appeal having been rejected with a clear indication that the ban was for life. I'd reached a crossroad. That sounded better than a dead end. With money inherited from my murdered part-time partner Lily Truscott I was ready to take off overseas for a while. See her brother fight in an elimination bout for a shot at the WBA welterweight title, travel around the States and Europe, drink with friends. Bringing down the people who'd killed Lily had helped with the grief and guilt, but I still had some things to come to terms with.

I'd found a handyman friend to sit my Glebe house while I was away and continue making some much-needed repairs.

Hank Bachelor, who'd helped me out more than once, was due to take over the Newtown office now that he'd got back his enthusiasm for the PEA business. A few hours before I was due to fly out business class, I went to the office to clean it up a bit. At least leave Hank some space in the filing cabinets.

A lot of the stuff could be hurled, some I'd take back home and stack away in a cupboard. I was sorting through it when I came across a thick folder that I hadn't touched in over twenty years. It was in a box of case files I'd moved from Darlinghurst to Newtown when St Peters Lane was targeted for renovation and rent rise.

The file with the words 'Hampshire Open' and the date '1988' scrawled across it was an inch—call it three centimetres—thick, unusual for me. My case files mostly didn't run much beyond a copy of the contract, my expense sheets, bank deposits and pages of scribbled notes, mostly illegible, from interviews. Photographs sometimes, photocopies, and microfilm and microfiche printouts in the old days. No internet downloads back then. Sometimes I included a few pages of the notes, diagrams and squiggles that I used to try to make sense of what was happening as things went along.

Reluctantly, I took the folder out of the box, slapped it on the desk and looked at it. It was dusty and musty and the blue folder was yellowed and crisp. Why was I punishing myself? I had money in the bank, was about to take a long overdue break. I'd been good at what I did until being good wasn't enough, and in this time of spin and protect your arse at all costs, I'd slipped up.

Back then I hadn't slipped up but I hadn't succeeded either. I opened the folder . . .

1

1987 I was sitting in my St Peters Lane office, reading about the $100 000 compensation being paid to the members of the Ananda Marga sect for wrongful imprisonment over the Hilton hotel bombing. They'd served seven years and a quick calculation told me that amounted to a bit over fourteen thousand a year. Not princely. They'd been fed and housed, but I doubted they were grateful. The pardon didn't surprise me: the little I'd had to do with security service types suggested that most of them would have had trouble passing a true or false test where the odds were even.

I put the paper aside when I heard the knock on the door and took my feet off the desk. I was expecting him, but he was late. I didn't like Paul Hampshire from the jump, and I never warmed to him. He came in trying to hide the fact that the two flights of stairs had put him out of breath. He wore a blue suit with a handkerchief in the jacket pocket and a bow tie. I've never trusted men who sport bow ties and handkerchiefs. I suppose they think it looks natty.

Anyway, nattiness was out of place in my office, which

could be described as drab although I preferred to think of it as functional. There were places to sit, places to put things. What else do you need? I could make coffee and I had a cask of red in a drawer and paper cups. A sixth-hand bar fridge kept the water, the white wine and the beer cold. The dirty windows made it a bit dim on a dull day, but that's kind of appropriate. The sunshine could struggle through at other times.

Hampshire had introduced himself over the phone an hour or so before and now he did it again in a loud voice, as if he needed to remind us both of who he was. I shook his hand—a bit soft, no sportsman, no gym-goer. He was tallish, but carrying too much weight, which accounted for the trouble with the stairs. There was something off about his sandy hair.

'I was told you'd seen military service,' he said. 'I prefer to deal with veterans, being one myself.'

He said this while still standing. He had the bearing and the moustache. I invited him to sit and he did, with only the barest glance of distaste at the chair. He didn't protect the creases in his trousers—that won him points, but he shot his cuffs, which lost them.

'What's the problem, Mr Hampshire?'

'Missing son. Mind if I smoke?' He had the cigarette out and the lighter up almost before I could make the appropriate response. I pushed an ashtray across the desk between us. He sucked on the cigarette and blew the smoke out in a cloud; he tapped on the edge of the ashtray but some of the ash didn't land in it—one of your dirty smokers. I made allowances for stress. I pulled a notepad towards me.

'Your son's name is?'

'Justin. He was seventeen and in his last year at school.'

Only just, I thought, *seeing that it was March. And why the past tense?* 'What's the name of the school?'

'Bryce Grammar, in Dee Why.'

I was a Maroubra High boy. My ex-wife, Cyn, who'd been to SCEGGS, kept in touch with her old school friends—Janey this had married Simon that of Shore, and Susie something had married Charles something else of Kings, and I'd overheard the gossip, but no mention of Bryce Grammar.

Hampshire was working through his cigarette as if time spent not puffing was time wasted. It was going to be a smoky interview. I wrote down the name of the school and encouraged him to give me the details. He lit more cigarettes, dropped more ash and visibly aged as he smoked and talked. He'd come in looking, say, fifty, and appeared more like sixty by the time he'd finished. But I had difficulty finding sympathy for him. I was sure that, convincing as some of it was, not everything he was telling me was the truth.

His son Justin was seventeen when he disappeared two years ago. Why was I being invited on board this late? Because Hampshire had been overseas, estranged from his wife and not really in touch with his son.

'I had a very big business deal in progress that needed my complete attention twenty-four seven, three hundred and sixty-five days a year. Plus I had . . . personal complications in the States. It was difficult. Angela is a hysteric. I never knew how much to believe and . . . time just slipped away.'

'But now you're back and concerned.'

'I was always concerned.'

'But busy.'

'I'm told you can be very provoking. I'm determined not to be provoked. I need your help, Mr Hardy.'

He butted his third cigarette and didn't light another to show how committed he was. He said his wife had reported their son's disappearance to the police and that all the usual procedures had been gone through.

'I'm not saying the police didn't take it seriously,' Hampshire said, 'but it wasn't the same as a ten-year-old schoolgirl. Justin was a big chap, about your size and build.'

That made him around 186 centimetres and 85 kilos—strapping for a teenager. I asked Hampshire for a photograph and he took one from his wallet. I wanted the photo but it's always nice to get a look at a wallet. Justin Hampshire was dark-haired, regular-featured, and wore a confident, head-up expression. He looked pretty much the way his father would have done before years, work and a fair bit of play had left their mark. Athletic? Probably. Intelligent? Hard to say, in both cases.

The kid was standing beside a car with P plates, looking proud. The car wasn't new but it wasn't a bomb—something Japanese and sporty, like a Honda Accord.

'I bought him the car just before I had to go over to the States. I taught him to drive in the times he stayed with me.'

That memory seemed to put a dent in his stoical recital. He fished for his cigarettes but stopped himself.

'You can smoke if it helps,' I said. 'This is going to be difficult and there's a lot more you're going to have to tell me—about the boy, about the marriage, your wife . . .'

'Ex-wife.'

'Right. Other family members here and people in America. Friends.'

'This has nothing to do with me in America.'

'How do you know he didn't go over to take a look, didn't like what he saw and took off for Alaska?'

'He was all set to go to Duntroon, family tradition. What you're saying's absurd.'

'Nothing's absurd in a missing person case, Mr Hampshire. Nothing's too good, nothing's too bad. I'm guessing he had a passport, from when you stumped up for a trip to . . . Bali? He can ski, right? He could be in Aspen, giving lessons.'

Hampshire stared at me. 'How could you know that?'

'I told you I was guessing.'

'It was Thailand, not Bali, but you're right, I paid for Justin and Angela and Sarah to go.'

'Sarah?'

'My daughter, I think. She's fifteen now.'

I added a note.

Hampshire ran a finger around the inside of his collar. *Take off the silly fucking tie*, I thought, but he didn't. His colour rose and he didn't look well. I got up and turned on a fan that moved the warm air around a little. I took a paper cup from the desk drawer, opened the bar fridge and poured him some cold water. He drank it down, undid the buttons on his jacket and leaned back in the chair.

'Thanks,' he said. 'I'm not in the best of shape—overweight, blood pressure. The pace of business over there is horrific.'

'I've seen the movies.'

'Yeah. And you're right again. Justin's an expert skier, in fact he's hell . . . I was going to say on two wheels, but that's not it. He surfs, snowboards—the things he could do on a skateboard would freeze your blood.'

'It freezes my blood to see them go over a gutter. It's coming through to me that you had a lot of feeling for your son.'

'I do. My God, I hadn't meant to go into all this. I thought I could just . . . but somehow you've . . .'

He really opened up then and it became clear that he was a man under a considerable amount of stress. His business deal in the US had gone sour along with a relationship he'd entered into there. The divorce had punitive alimony provisions and he more or less admitted that he'd done a flit. I'd seen it before—marry or partner up on the rebound, get bounced and go back to where you started, or try to.

'I got in touch with Angela when I arrived back. I thought . . . but she didn't want to know. Didn't want me to see Sarah. I should've known how much Justin's disappearance had affected her but I didn't. I'm not the most sensitive man in the world. That's why I'm here now. If I can show that I'm doing something about Justin, however late, and if you can find him . . .'

'I won't kid you,' I said. 'Two years is a long gap. So much can happen.'

His mouth turned down. 'Don't I just know it.'

He was a strange mixture of cockiness and distress, self-esteem and self-reproach. But if I'd waited for a straightforward client I'd be sitting in my office bending and straightening paperclips for a long time. I got as much as I could from him—his ex-wife's address and phone number, the location of Bryce Grammar, the name of the police officer who'd stayed in touch with Angela Hampshire through the active search time. I didn't push for details about his experiences in America. Maybe later if it became necessary.

He signed a contract and gave me his contact details. He was living in a serviced apartment in Rose Bay. He wrote me a cheque. Doing that seemed to restore his confidence.

'How will you proceed, Mr Hardy?'

First off I'll deposit the cheque, I thought, but I said, 'I'll have to talk to the former Mrs Hampshire.'

'Please do. At least she'll know I'm doing something.'

'Are you still in touch with her?'

'Brief phone calls.'

'What about Sarah?'

He shook his head.

'How are you occupying yourself now?'

'I have investments to manage, and legal matters to negotiate.'

'This could be expensive.'

He sighed. 'What isn't?'

'How did you hear about me?'

'I read a newspaper report about a matter you were involved in. It was hardly flattering, but it mentioned your military service and your reputation for persistence.'

'It didn't say anything about how brainy and honest I am.'

Hampshire almost smiled. 'I checked on that with a police acquaintance. He said that you liked to . . . take the piss.'

'This is a difficult and serious matter, Mr Hampshire. I'll give it serious attention.'

We shook hands and he left. I sat at the desk and made a closer examination of the photograph of young Hampshire. He was big, with a heaviness to his neck and shoulders that suggested he'd be bulky in later life. He didn't look anything like his father but that didn't mean much. My father was fair and on the small side. Justin looked healthy and untroubled, but a lot can be going on under the surface in an adolescent—family trouble, girl trouble, boy trouble. Maybe he didn't want to go to Duntroon. Maybe he wanted to try out for NIDA or the Sydney Dance Company. Good set of shoulders on him, probably just right for skiing. I hoped I didn't track him to some snowfield. I hate the cold.

The newspaper report Hampshire had mentioned was about a fraud involving counterfeiting and blackmail. I'd spent nearly six months on it—hunting people down, unravelling the connections. It had ended with me putting a man in hospital and almost being charged with assault. But the good outcome had overridden that. The bonus was useful, the publicity wasn't. The headline on the page three item had been something like 'Private Eye goes too far', but it had caught Hampshire's attention. The report was almost a year old, published when Hampshire, according to what he'd told me, was still in America. It wouldn't have got a run in the *New York Times*, the *LA Times* or the *San Francisco Chronicle*. He must have been reading the *Sydney Morning Herald*. Despite his troubles, still calling Australia home.

2

I got to the bank in time to deposit the cheque. Funds were low so it'd be a help when it cleared. *If* it cleared. Clients imagine you can just drop everything and hop straight into the job they've given you, but it wasn't like that. I had another matter on hand I had to see through and if young Hampshire had been missing for two years, another day before I got on his trail wasn't going to make much difference.

There are quite a few cases on record of men faking death for one reason or another—to allow someone to claim insurance, to escape from financial troubles, like the British MP Stonehouse who turned up here after disappearing from an American beach, or out of a simple wish to start all over again. They're still not sure about Lord Lucan and some of the smart money says he's in Kenya without his moustache. I hope they catch him; a more useless human being I never heard of. But it's very unusual for a woman to play this game, and that was the case I'd been working on for some time.

Melanie Hastings was a businesswoman importing Taiwanese-made clothing, screens and decorative fans. She was in comfortable, but not affluent, circumstances. She apparently vanished while on a skiing trip. A storm had blown up and her party had got into difficulties. The party consisted of Ms Hastings, a friend named Brenda Costello and their guide and instructor, Helmut Manne. The guide and Ms Costello made it to a hut but no trace was found of Melanie Hastings. Her life had been insured for four hundred thousand dollars, and the beneficiary was her friend Ms Costello.

'That was the clever part,' Tom Cooper said.

Cooper was an American who'd come to Australia after visiting on R & R during the Vietnam War. He'd married an Australian and set up a go-getting, fast-tracking, low-overhead insurance business, among other things. He'd taken Melanie Hastings's business because the insurance 'product' he was offering included very high premiums. Cooper didn't employ a full-time investigator, and he'd contacted me on the recommendation of a satisfied client. He was brash and ambitious and not given to any sentimentality.

'What's that Aussie expression? Means spotting a sucker.'

'She saw you coming,' I said.

'That's it.' He sat back in the chair in his austere office and laughed. You couldn't help liking him. The pay-out would hurt him badly, but he was sort of enjoying the dramatics. That's rare when big money is involved.

I'd worked for an insurance company in the past, mainly as an investigator of arson claims. This was beyond my experience. 'You mentioned cleverness,' I said.

'Right. It didn't take long for the cops to find out that Brenda and Helmut were an item. Motive for disposing of

Melanie obvious, but there was no evidence. Not a single person thought there was any hostility between the two dames. Both Brenda and Helmut passed lie detector tests—for what they're worth: *Did you kill Melanie? No*. Needle doesn't jump.

'It's a fucking snowfield. What're the cops going to do? They wait until the snow melts, although it's a cool summer and it doesn't melt all that much and they keep making the artificial stuff. They dig around. Nothing. I'm looking at a big loss, a doozy. Won't break me but won't help.'

'Don't seven years have to elapse before someone can be declared dead?'

Cooper thumped the desk. 'In theory! But a good lawyer can work around it and guess what Brenda's profession is?'

'I get it,' I said. 'So they've pulled it off. Too bad.'

'Oh, no.' Cooper wagged his finger. 'Ever seen the movie *Double Indemnity*?'

'Of course,' I said. 'A few times.'

'I've had a feeling about this all along. I knew something was wrong but I couldn't put my finger on it. But now I have.'

'You've got me interested and I can charge you for the time, but I can't see how I can help you.'

He snapped his fingers and the red braces he wore over his whiter-than-white shirt and let go his infectious grin. 'Brenda was the beard.'

He meant, as anyone who's seen a Woody Allen film or read American fiction would know, that the real relationship was between Melanie Hastings and Helmut Manne and that Brenda, as we'd say here, was a front.

'How d'you know that?' I said.

'I don't know it. I feel it. I want you to find out if it's true.'

So I dug as deep as I'd ever done into the backgrounds of all three people—talking to neighbours, friends, clients, acquaintances and conducting surveillance on Brenda and Helmut. Their relationship looked pretty tepid to me, and my enquiries revealed that Helmut's type was nothing like Brenda, who was dark, sturdily built and athletic. Helmut preferred the slender blondes who had need of his strength. That description more closely fitted Melanie. It wasn't an exact fit, but Melanie had the added attraction of money. Helmut had had a few gigolo episodes in his time.

All this was suggestive and nothing more until one of the acquaintances happened to mention Melanie's interest in plastic surgery: 'I mean it was crazy. She wasn't old. She didn't need it. But we were drinking, fooling around. She said there was someone in South Australia who could do it without needing a referral from a doctor.'

Mike Trent, a colleague, if we PEAs can use that word, in Adelaide knew about Dr Heinrich Manne and things began to fall into place. He was Helmut's uncle. I flew to Adelaide and, with Mike's help, broke into Manne's office. His files contained before and after pictures of his clients and I had no trouble spotting Melanie Hastings. She was living in a flat in the suburbs, keeping a very low profile.

I flew back to Sydney and told Cooper all about it.

'I knew it. Am I good or what?'

'Brilliant, but you've got a problem—extradition.'

'Say what?'

'If she's arrested in South Australia she'd have to be extradited to face the charges here. That could take a while.

A lawyer could really tie it up, especially as there'd be questions about identity.'

'Jesus wept. So what do we do?'

We turned our minds to ways of luring her back to Sydney. We couldn't make any use of Brenda or Helmut because that'd be sure to spook her. In desperation, Cooper suggested an outright kidnap.

'That'd really give the lawyers a field day.'

'A field day?'

'You're going to have to learn the lingo, Tom. A picnic.'

'I get it. Well, my news is that Brenda's applied to have the will probated. They tell me that's the way to speed up the process of getting Melanie declared dead. That'll put me under pressure to pay up, so I might just have to take the lawyers' heat.'

As it turned out Melanie, now calling herself Marci Holden, was heading back to Sydney without being lured. Mike Trent was keeping a watching brief and he saw her go to the agent handling her flat and, posing as a prospective tenant, found out when she was leaving and her destination. He stayed in contact and let us know when she was on her way to the airport.

Tom and I had spoken to the detective in charge of the initial investigation and put him in the picture more or less day by day and now hour by hour. He arranged to arrest Melenie aka Marci on her arrival and Tom insisted that I be there to see it went smoothly.

'I don't trust cops,' he said.

'This one's all right,' I said. 'I think.'

'Be there.'

*

That's what I had to finish off before taking on Paul Hampshire's case. I met up with Detective Sergeant Philip Harper and saw him arrest the woman who had a more shapely nose, tighter skin, blonder hair and a slimmer figure than the original Melanie. It went as smoothly as a Navratilova forehand.

Tom Cooper congratulated me when I phoned him and said he'd pay me as soon as he'd straightened out some accounting problems. I'd heard that before and I'd used up his retainer. I had a quiet celebration with a few mates in the Toxteth pub, but, with a mortgage to pay, office rent due and liability insurance always a burden, I had to press on with the next earner.

The following day, I rang the serviced apartments in Rose Bay and asked for Hampshire. The concierge, or whatever he was called, tried the number with no result. At least I knew he lived there. I rang the number Hampshire had given me for his ex-wife. The woman who answered had the sort of voice that conjured images of pony clubs and garden parties. I stated my business.

'Well at least and at last he's doing something. What do you want from me, Mr Hardy?'

'A meeting, a discussion, details about Justin. Your authority to interview people at the school . . .'

'Couldn't you have got that from him?'

'I forgot to ask.'

'That's not encouraging.'

'There's a lot of ground to cover, Mrs Hampshire.'

'Pettigrew, Ms—I've gone back to my maiden name.'

'Are you still living where you lived when Justin was with you?'

'Yes, why?'

'I'd like to look at his . . . things.'

'The police looked at them. They weren't any help.'

'I'd be looking from a different angle. And I'd like to have a talk with Sarah if possible.'

'Are you expensive, Mr Hardy?'

'Not particularly.'

'Pity. Very well. Sarah will be home from school at three thirty. Shall we say four o'clock tomorrow?'

It sounded as if I'd better wear a jacket and mind my manners. I was beginning to see signs of the problems in the Hampshire nuptials. Paul was basically smooth but there were traces of rough edges here and there. And he'd dropped the hint about the questionable paternity of the daughter. Angela sounded genuinely top drawer. Either that or she was a good actress. She didn't sound like a hysteric. And I was reminded of the quote from Willie Pep, the much-married boxer: 'All my wives was great housekeepers. They always kept the house.'

My second last call was to Detective Sergeant Stefan Gunnarson of the Missing Persons Division. We'd had dealings before.

'You again,' he said.

'Me again, to help you close a file.'

'Hah, well, you did once.'

'Twice.'

'Have it your way. Okay, who?'

'A few years back—Justin Hampshire, seventeen.'

'Shit, a nightmare mother and an absent father.'

'Clear in your memory, that's good. Can I come in and see what you've got? How about tomorrow, in the morning? As I said to the lady, there's a lot of ground to cover.'

'She got you in?'

'No, I spoke to the ex on the phone. The father hired me. He's back from the land of the brave and the home of the free.'

Gunnarson snorted. 'Well, that's something. We were lucky to get a fax out of the fucker. When you meet the missus you'll understand why he went twelve thousand fucking miles away. Okay, Hardy, eleven thirty, don't be late.'

Always good to have a few bookings for the day ahead, even if they were spread out. Gunnarson was in Darlinghurst and Ms Pettigrew was up at Church Point. But I was on expenses, wasn't I?

I got through to the registrar's secretary at Bryce Grammar. After a little difficulty, she arranged to fit me in at the earliest opportunity—the morning of the day after next. She confirmed that I'd need parental authorisation.

I had a few small things to clean up and some to put on hold—faxes, phone calls, cheques in the mail. It was late when I got home and the house was hot after the muggy day. I ate some leftover cold chicken and salad and went to bed with the ceiling fan working overtime. I read a few pages of Robert Hughes's *The Fatal Shore*. I had English and French settlers on my father's side, according to research by my sister. Solidly Irish on my mother's, with a few convicts—cutpurses and streetwalkers, nothing romantic, no land grantees or rum dealers. There was no Hardytown or Hardy Flats, but Hardys'd been here from early on and that mattered to me in reflective moments. I reached the chapter on 'Bolters and Bushrangers' and closed the book. The fan clattered a bit but I slept.

Stefan Gunnarson was no one's idea of a Scandinavian. He was short and dark and he sweated a lot. His division was housed in a series of small connecting rooms in the Surry Hills police complex and it was the usual jumble of makeshift partitions, filing cabinets, desks, whiteboards and stacks of paper. Gunnarson had a cubicle slightly bigger than the others and slightly apart—the only signifier of his rank. He'd told me previously that he reported to people 'upstairs' who had carpet on their floors.

My pass was marked with the date and 'AM'. I fingered it as I sat down opposite him.

'Will I turn into a pumpkin at twelve oh-one?'

'That'd be your famous charm at work, would it? You're wearing a clean shirt and pants and that jacket was dry-cleaned recently. Let me guess. You're on your way to see the dragon lady of Church Point.'

'Right.'

'Good luck.' He had a thick spring-back folder on the desk and he released the contents. 'Can't show you the whole thing for obvious reasons, but I can give you the flavour.'

He sorted through the documents, withholding some and passing others across. I read the initial report and statements from Justin's mother and sister. A couple of the neighbours had also been interviewed and some of the boy's friends. The police had followed up on a few of the matters raised—a surf carnival up the coast at around the relevant time, a ski lodge where Justin had stayed a year before he disappeared. A draft copy of his letter of application to Duntroon Military Academy had been found in his wastepaper basket, torn in half. The two pages were now sticky taped together.

Gunnarson watched me as I read through it. The letter was correctly spelt, the grammar was accurate and the points were made clearly.

'Torn in half,' I said.

'What do you do with drafts?'

'Crumple them or use them as scrap paper.'

Gunnarson shrugged.

I read three faxes from Hampshire in California. In the first he said he was coming back, in the next he claimed to be delayed, in the third he said he couldn't make it due to business commitments but would write supplying every detail about his son he could summon up.

'Where's the letter?'

'Never arrived.'

'Did you contact the Californian cops?'

'You think we're amateurs? Of course we did. Hampshire was up to his balls in complicated real estate deals. Legitimate but involving . . .' He snapped his fingers. 'What's that finance crap young Warwick Fairfax stuffed up over?'

'Junk bonds, whatever they are.'

'Right. But there was no sign he was harbouring a runaway son.'

'Still, the kid had a passport.'

'We checked the ports, and I mean sea and air. Nothing. And nothing from New Zealand where he could've gone without a passport and used it as a jumping off point, in case that was what you were going to ask. Sorry, but we didn't feel a need to bring in Interpol.'

I shuffled the papers in front of me. 'Nothing from the school here.'

'We talked to some students and some teachers but, you

know, private school, sensitive parents, lawyers from arsehole to breakfast. Can't show you any of that.'

'But no useful leads?'

'Nope. The kid shaped up as Master Clean.'

'So what d'you think happened, Sarge? Speculate.'

'I haven't a clue. Like it says, he took off in his Honda on a Saturday morning before anyone else at home got up. He took a few clothes and other bits and pieces. Sold his skis and his surfboard and skateboard and snowboard the week before. The kid was a balance-at-speed freak. It's a wonder he didn't have rollerblades and ice skates. He bought petrol locally and that's the last anyone saw of him or the car.'

'No bodies've turned up, no burnt-out Hondas?'

Gunnarson shook his head. 'He could be scallop fishing in Bass Strait or riding the fucking rabbit-proof fence.'

'You don't think he came to harm?'

'It's possible of course, but he was a well set-up kid with a fair bit of money. No history of drugs or dodgy behaviour, and he'd obviously planned it. Turned eighteen within a few months of leaving. An adult.'

'Did you ask yourself why?'

'Over and over. The way you will.'

I made some notes from the papers I'd been allowed to see, thanked Gunnarson and left. Way too early for any theories, but not for being thoroughly intrigued.

It was after one pm when I left the police building with my permit well and truly expired. Time to fill in before the appointment in Church Point. It was not an area I was familiar with—I'd have to do some work in the *Gregory's.* I decided I'd earned some food and went to a pub in

William Street where they did a fair counter lunch. Like all the best old pubs they had sporting pictures on the walls and the bar staff were mature, friendly females.

I bought a middy of Old and ordered the shepherd's pie. I wished Gunnarson had let me photocopy some of the papers I'd seen but he drew the line at that. He had to protect his arse against any fallout, and that headline about me and threat of a charge hadn't boosted my standing with the cops. Working fast, I'd tried for a verbatim copy of Hampshire's faxes but, when I opened my notebook, I found parts of my scrawl hard to read.

The food came and, as I ate and drank, I stared at the notes I'd made of the faxes. There was a formality about some of the phrases—'busy as I am', 'anxious to assist', but also a defensiveness—'I raised my son to be resourceful', 'he may need a period of relief from his mother's excessive protectiveness'.

I was finishing up when Gunnarson walked into the pub, looked around, spotted me and came over.

'Thought I might find you here,' he said.

'You've found him and I'm out of a job.'

'Funny. No, Hampshire contacted the wife, she contacted social services, who contacted us. He's way behind on his maintenance payments for the daughter.' He put a card beside my plate. 'Here's the number to report his whereabouts. I'll leave it up to you.'

'Why?'

'Two reasons. I suppose you've got a fighting chance of finding the kid and that'd clear a case for me and be good all round. And I'm divorced with an ex from hell. My guess is, that Hampshire bitch would gouge his eyes out and sell them to get square with him.'

He nodded and walked away. I put the card in my pocket and thought about what Gunnarson had said as I strolled back to the car. The last thing I needed was Hampshire under economic stress—bad for him, bad for me, bad, potentially, for Justin. Not a big ethical dilemma, but I needed to hear Angela Pettigrew's story before making any hard and fast decisions. I filled the tank and kept the receipt to go on Hampshire's bill. Three days for the cheque to clear—that could have a bearing on things. Hampshire had mentioned investments—I hoped his stocks were rising.

I hadn't been over to the north side for some time and, as always, they'd shifted the lanes on the bridge so that I had to keep my wits about me to be in position for the turn-offs. Midafternoon and the traffic was light, which made it easier. I picked up Pittwater Road in North Manly and just kept on going, with Joni Mitchell on the cassette player:

I'm gonna see the folks I dig,
I'll even kiss a sunset pig . . .

What the hell was a sunset pig?

Pittwater is spectacular country with the beaches, the high bluffs and the islands. A boatie's paradise and there seemed to be plenty of people around with the money to indulge the passion. Boats of all sizes, from the Greg Norman style craft swinging gently at the deep water moorings to tinnies tied to jetties and rocks, bobbing in the shallows. The water was grey under a heavy sky; the high masts and trees swayed to a strong breeze.

The address was on Captain Hunter Road overlooking McCarrs Creek towards Ku-ring-gai Chase National Park. The road bent slightly at that point and I parked a little further on. The house was a large, rambling weatherboard set high on a big bushy block with a winding, stepped path climbing up to it. The climb would certainly test Paul Hampshire's wind now, as it did mine, but presumably he was fitter when he first moved in, which must have been more than twenty years ago. At that time, with the distance from Sydney and the rough roads, perhaps the house wasn't too expensive. It would have more than doubled its value now and be on the rise as the people with the Mercs and the boats moved in.

Near the beginning of the path the hill had been dug into to make a carport. No car. The path was showing signs of wear and tear and sections of the handrail were shaky. I made it up to the deep verandah that ran across the front of the house and looked back. The view—the sky, the water, the bush—smacked you in the eye. I opened the unlatched flywire screen, which had a slight tear in the mesh, and knocked on the door. I'd expected a tall, cool blonde with high cheekbones, maybe because of listening to Joni. The woman who appeared was nothing like that. She was shortish, compact and dark, but she still had the plummy voice. She wasn't the school's netball captain or freestyle star—perhaps the top debater and certainly a prefect.

'Mr Hardy, do come in. We'll go through to the sunroom. Not that there's much of it today. Dreadful weather.'

I didn't think it was so bad, but up here, I guessed you expected the best at all times. We went down polished boards, past a series of rooms on either side of the long hallway, through a flagstoned kitchen to a partially glassed-in balcony that hung out over an overgrown lawn and neglected garden. The floors were swept and the surfaces shone but the outside needed work. Rude of me to notice.

'Would you care for tea, Mr Hardy?'

Tea? You'd have to hold me down and use a funnel. 'No, thanks, Ms Pettigrew.'

'Please sit.'

We sat on padded cane chairs. She wore a blouse and skirt, medium heels. She had good legs. No wedding ring, no jewellery. She had disconcertingly dark eyes that bulged just slightly, making you feel watched more closely than you wanted to be. Her complexion was pale and smooth with just a few lines showing. If she wore makeup it was subtle. She was just short of attractive but certainly interesting-looking and that can be better.

'I've spoken to your former husband, obviously,' I said, 'and to the policeman who supervised the investigation into your missing son.'

'Gunnarson,' she said. 'Competent, I thought, but nothing beyond that.'

'I believe I need your authority to talk to people at the school.' I took a sheet from my pocket. 'I typed up something appropriate. Would you mind signing it?'

She glanced at it briefly and signed with the pen I offered.

'I wanted to ask you about Justin—his habits his character, I suppose. As I said, I'd like to look at what he left behind and to hear any thoughts you might have about what caused him to leave.'

She inclined her head slightly. 'To leave? That's an interesting way of putting it. Yes, I rather like that. He left, didn't he?'

There was a quality to her I couldn't put my finger on. Call it a lack of frankness, a feeling that much was being held back. But it was impossible to tell whether this related to Justin or to something else. Her degree of composure was disconcerting and I had a sense that she knew I was aware of it and was playing me. I began to get an inkling of what Gunnarson had meant by 'dragon lady'. I didn't want to be played. Time to be direct.

'D'you think he's still alive, Ms Pettigrew?'

'Very possibly not, and if so it's all Paul's fault, the coward.'

3

I was about to probe that remark when the front door slammed and I heard laughter and pounding footsteps in the hallway. Angela Pettigrew shot out of her chair as if released by a spring and went quickly through the kitchen to the passage, heels clacking on the boards. I followed and her voice, raised to a shout but still with the rounded vowels, echoed through the space.

'Sarah! Who do you have with you? Come out of there at once!'

By the time we reached the door it had opened and a young man had come out looking alarmed and disoriented. He turned towards us, realised he was headed the wrong way, pushed Ms Pettigrew aside and made her lose balance. She fell and swore.

A younger female voice screeched, 'No, Ronny!'

Ronny was big, young and frightened and he made the mistake of throwing a punch at me as he tried to get clear. I blocked his clumsy swing with my left forearm and hooked him low in the ribs with a short right, the way I'd done hundreds of times in the ring. A skilful boxer spots it early and sways away, reducing the impact. Ronny didn't know the moves and the punch took the wind out of him and rubberised his legs. He went down in a heap as Ms Pettigrew got gamely and smoothly to her feet.

Sarah, all teased blonde hair and eye makeup, stood in the doorway in her bra and school skirt and giggled as I helped steady her mother, who accepted the support momentarily and then brushed me off like a troublesome fly.

'Who's this, then, *Mummy?* Nice!'

Give her her due, Angela was up to the job. She stepped forward, landed a heavy slap on the girl's face, shoved her back inside the room and pulled the door shut. She wasn't even breathing hard. She'd be good on the steps. Maybe she had made the hockey team.

'You hypocritical bitch!' the girl screamed.

Ronny was sucking in air and pressing himself back against the wall, trying to slide upright.

'You,' Angela said, completely under control now and nudging Ronny with her foot. 'Get out!'

He scrambled up, all legs and arms in jeans, sneakers and bomber jacket, and rushed to the door. His fly zipper was still undone. Rock music came from inside the room.

'Well,' Ms Pettigrew said, 'after all that I don't suppose there's any use pretending we're a happy family.'

'Not many are all the time.'

'I suppose not. She looked at her watch and tapped the side of her head with an index finger. 'Oh, I've got it now—I told her I'd be away having the car seen to until late, but as it turned out I had to have it towed. I forgot to tell her about my appointment with you. I have to admit I was going to cancel it in favour of dealing with the car, until it wouldn't start and it became clear from the NRMA person that it was undriveable and so I'd still be here to see you. She . . . they obviously thought I wasn't here. I must say you were quick and . . . decisive.'

So were you, I thought, but I didn't say it. 'He was just a boy, no experience.'

On the way back to the sunroom she stopped in the kitchen, swivelled, and headed towards a drinks tray on a pine sideboard. 'I'm going to have a whisky. Would you care for one, Mr Hardy?'

'I would. Thank you.'

'Ice?'

'Just water.'

'Quite right.' She poured two solid belts of Cutty Sark, added water from a cooler and took the drinks through to where we'd been sitting.

'Cheers, and thank you for your help. That big lump of a boy could have hurt me.'

'He was more frightened than anything else, but he did need discouraging.'

She smiled. 'You do have a nice way of putting things. Sarah is an uncontrolled and uncontrollable little hoyden. I don't know what I'm going to do with her. She's been on the brink of expulsion from St Margaret's many a time.'

'Unlike Justin.'

'My word, yes. He was an exemplary . . . oh God.' She took a strong pull on her drink and stroked the side of her face with her free hand. 'I must have sounded so cold before. It's the way I was brought up. Don't show your feelings, remain in control. I do, but sometimes I want to scream.'

I drank some scotch and gave her a minute, then I said, 'You've got a lot on your hands. I'll only ask one question and then I'd like to see anything of Justin's you can show me. What did you mean when you said his disappearance was your husband's fault?'

She knocked back the rest of her drink. 'Paul had always gone on about the military tradition of the Hampshires—the Boer War, World Wars I and II and all that, plus his own service in Vietnam. He filled Justin to the brim with the idea of Duntroon and the military. Justin and I had an argument about something or other and I told him that Paul had served briefly as a supply officer in Vietnam before being invalided out. He never fired a shot in anger or had one fired at him, never left the base. This was after Paul had deserted us, making noises about American business deals, promising to look into scholarships to West Point.'

'So Justin . . . ?'

'I'm guessing. He and I never spoke about . . . personal matters, not really, not manly—you know? I'm guessing he went off to do something brave, unlike his father, to prove to him and himself that he was a man. God knows what, and he hasn't been heard of since . . .'

Her pain was palpable now but I had to ask one more question. 'Did you tell any of this to the police?'

'No, I was ashamed of the mess we were in and it was just a guess. What good could it do?'

I had the feeling that she wanted to say a lot more but couldn't bring herself to do it. She lowered her dark head, strands of grey showing at the crown, and pointed. 'Second door on the right is Justin's room. Take all the time you need. Thank you again, Mr Hardy. I'm going to lie down.'

*

I didn't recognise the music coming from behind Sarah's door and didn't want to. Justin's room wasn't one of those shrines to the departed you hear about. It had been tidied and I had the impression a good deal of the paraphernalia had been removed. It was basically just a bedroom with posters on the walls—standard teenage stuff—and marks where other stuff had been stuck, perhaps too affecting to be allowed to stay.

There wasn't much in the desk and didn't look as if there ever had been—no diary, nothing taped to the underside of a drawer, no hollowed-out cavities. A bookshelf held a few textbooks—history, English, human movement, agricultural science—and there was a well overdue school library copy of Serle's biography of Monash along with paperbacks of Waugh's *Put Out More Flags* and a couple of Clancys and Forsyths. Oh for the days of blotters with indiscretions scribbled on them and discarded carbon papers. A calendar for the year Justin went missing was taped to the side of the bookcase, effectively hidden from view. The date of his mother's missing person report was 18 September. The date the HSC exams were to start was circled in red, but further back, on 1 August, was scribbled 'Ag Sci Ex'.

I took the Serle book down and something fell out from it—a reader's ticket to the Mitchell Library. I left the room and knocked quietly on the door almost opposite. No response. I knocked louder and the music stopped.

'What?'

'I'm a private investigator looking into the disappearance of your brother. I want to talk to you.'

'Fuck off.'

'Any message if I run into Ronny?'

'Tell him to fuck off, too.' The music kicked in—loud!

I went back to the sunroom, drained my scotch and left my card near the glass. I had to hope Sarah wouldn't tear it up.

It was raining, making the steps treacherous. I went down gingerly and hurried to the car. A U-turn and I was back heading south, away from the big houses and boats that are no protection against the worst kinds of trouble. A couple of hundred metres along I spotted Ronny. He was hunched up inside his jacket, with one hand in his pocket and the other thumbing for a ride. Seemed to be favouring his right side a little. I drove a short way past, stopped and opened the door. He got in and grunted his thanks before he identified me. By then I'd reached across him to close the door and had the car moving.

'Take it easy,' I said, 'it's pissing down. You need a lift and I need to talk to you.'

The rain was lashing the windscreen now, the wipers barely coping. He shoved both hands into his pockets and gave me a stare that was supposed to be hard but ended up sullen. 'Who are you, then? The mother's new bloke?'

I told him who I was and what I was doing as I drove carefully on the narrow road. His only response was a shrug. On closer inspection, he was a presentable kid—tall, lean and dark, trying for a beard and not quite making it yet. His clothes were the standard uniform but not bargain basement—New Balance high-tops—and he wore an expensive-looking watch. He examined the interior of the old Falcon and was unimpressed.

'Have you got a smoke?' he said.

'You might find some in the glove-box.'

He opened it up and took out a crumpled packet of Marlboros. 'Three in it.'

'You can have 'em,' I said. 'And the lighter. Someone left them behind.'

He put a cigarette in his mouth.

'You can smoke when you get out and after you answer a few questions. Okay?'

He wanted to ask me what Sarah had told me but with the rain pelting and the cigarettes available he decided to play it cool. Me too.

'You need to learn a bit about fighting, son. You had a go, which I admire, but you should always keep your head moving and punch for the body. Bigger target.'

The cigarette in his mouth jiggled as he nodded. 'If you say so.'

'And you shouldn't have pushed the woman. I know you were scared—'

'Who says I'm scared?'

'I do. You're scared a lot of the time. I was at your age. How far're you going?'

'Mona Vale.'

'I'll drop you. Did you know Sarah's brother, Justin?'

'Yeah, I knew him. Went to the same fucking school until they chucked me out.'

'What was he like?'

'He was an arsehole.'

'Explain.'

'Always crapping on about the heroes in his fucking family. Grandfather and great-grandfather dying in battle, how he was going to be an officer and all that shit. Who cares?'

'What else?'

'He used to try to protect Sarah from blokes like me. Not that she wanted protection, and when he pissed off, wow, did she cut loose.'

'Still at school, isn't she?'

He sniggered and pushed up the sleeve of his jacket to scratch at a new-looking tattoo of an image I couldn't identify. 'Not a lot. Look, she basically goes for the drama classes. She wants to be a fucking actress and she's acting all the time. Anyhow, she wasn't at school today. We thought her old lady was out till late.'

'Any more to tell me?'

'No. Yeah, that car. Man, if I had a car like that what wouldn't I do, but him—went fucking surfing and skiing and even went down to Canberra to look at some fucking museum. Nerd.'

'When was this?'

'Not long before he went, or whatever.'

'Have you got any theory on that?'

'What d'you mean?'

'What do you think happened to him?'

The shrug and the snigger. 'Dunno and don't care. Sarah reckons he went off to be a soldier's fortune, whatever the fuck that is.'

'Soldier of fortune. A mercenary, fighting for money.'

Ronny had nothing to say to that one way or the other. We drove on in silence for a while as the rain eased.

'What do you do, Ronny?'

'Nothing much. Stop here.'

I pulled over and he got out. It looked for a second as if he intended to slam the door, but he glanced in at me and thought better of it.

It was late in the day. Bryce Grammar was in North Narrabeen and I was more or less on the spot. No reason to cross the harbour back to an empty house that might, if the rain had been falling in Glebe, be leaking. I booked into a Mona Vale motel—another charge on my client—ate a meal at a nearby Vietnamese restaurant and returned to watch some TV and make notes and squiggles on what I was beginning to think of—after Ronny's slack-minded reference to Justin's grandfather and great-grandfather—as the Hampshire saga. My recall for conversation wasn't perfect but it was pretty good. A remark of Ronny's stuck in my mind: *Are you the mother's new bloke? New?*

Something had happened to send Justin Hampshire—focused, solid student set on a solid career, protector of his sister, adept sportsman—off in a spin. What? His mother had suggested disappointment at learning of his father's indifferent military career and desertion. Possible, but it seemed a bit thin. Where he was certainly had to do with why he went. Angela Pettigrew's acceptance of the possibility that her son could be dead worried me. Did mothers have an instinct about such things? How would I know?

I worked the mini-bar a bit—not a client expense—and wished I'd brought the Hughes book as bedtime reading. I read bits and pieces of the Serle biography of Monash instead and that was useful. Someone—Justin?—had underlined certain passages about the AIF's heroic and sacrificial struggles at the Somme.

4

I didn't sleep well. I had one of those nights when you wake up every hour or so for no reason you can fathom—not snoring, no outside noise, no bladder pressure. At four am I gave up, turned on the television and switched it off after flicking through the channels. Radio National was replaying a program on experimental music. I was reminded of the remark a music critic had made about a revival of the musical *Jesus Christ, Superstar*: 'If you missed it the first time, here's a chance to miss it again'.

I made a cup of coffee, read for a bit and then put the book down. Of course I found myself thinking about the case, going over the twists and turns. I wasn't sure exactly how many missing person cases I'd worked on or what my strike rate was, but I knew it was in positive territory. This had the feel of a hard one—the background, the family circumstances, the deceptions and disappointments provided complex motives for the disappearance and equally complex directions for the detective to follow.

The welcome morning light started to creep into the room and the feeling I always get in those conditions—a mixture of loneliness and relief at being my own master

—left me in a meditative mood. A question that had been wafting around, half-formed, came into focus. Why had Angela Pettigrew married Paul Hampshire? She appeared to have come from a more favourable background, was more physically attractive or interesting, and certainly smarter.

You could have fitted the whole of Maroubra High—buildings, playground, assembly area, the lot—four or five times into the space occupied by Bryce Grammar. The grass on the playing fields was green; the artificial turf on the tennis courts had that eerie shine; the paths were gravel and there were parking areas for both students and staff. The flowerbeds were out of *Home & Garden,* and the buildings, though not very old, had already acquired a becoming amount of ivy in all the right places.

The classroom buildings were at a distance and I could see some blazered students walking around and sitting under shade. There was no one batting, bowling or hitting—it was evidently a serious time of the day on a serious day of the week. I went up some imposing sandstone steps into the carpeted quietness of the administration building and found the office of the registrar. His secretary was a cheerful, plump, middle-aged woman who asked me to wait while she took my note of authority in to the boss. That occupied enough time for me to look around and get some idea of what the registrar actually did to need a secretary and a day and a bit before he could see someone. The photographs of men and women in suits told the story—he lobbied and raised money from old boys and anyone else he could put the touch on.

The secretary came back minus the letter and ushered me past her cubicle to a door with 'A R McKenzie-Brown, Registrar' on a laminated card in a slot. Bit of a worry those slots—a name that can be slotted in can easily be slotted out. To my surprise the occupant opened the door at her knock and thanked her before stepping aside and beckoning me in. A lot of self-important executive types like to be seen working at their desks when you arrive. Looking busy. Not McKenzie-Brown. He was a tall, lean type in his early forties—shirt-sleeves, loosened tie, cigarette in hand. He offered me the other hand.

'Mr Hardy, hello. Come in and have a seat. Belinda'll have coffee here in a moment whether you want it or not, because *I* want it.'

I shook his hand. Was it an act? Hard to tell, but if so it was a good one. Couldn't help but like him—provisionally. I sat down; he stubbed out the cigarette and shuffled a pile of papers on his desk.

'Belinda will make a copy of the note from Ms Pettigrew—I see she's reverted to her maiden name—for our records. I'm sure you'll want the original for yours. Now, I've assembled as many reports and assessments and such as I could lay my hands on. They're pretty uniform actually. Justin was an excellent student and you'll see the phrase "A pleasure to have in the class" or something like it pretty often. Ah, here's the coffee. I'll just get on with a few things while you look this over.'

Belinda brought in two mugs of coffee, a bowl of sugar and a jug of milk. McKenzie-Brown thanked her and handed her the Pettigrew note. I tasted the coffee—strong and good, didn't need milk or sugar. McKenzie-Brown took both and stirred vigorously.

It didn't take long to get the measure of Justin Hampshire's performance—he was consistently in the top few in every subject. Particularly good at history and agricultural science, which seemed like an odd combination, but what do I know? He won prizes, played cricket and tennis in the school teams, led the student group on skiing trips. He'd been his class monitor pretty well all the way through and was vice-head prefect in his final year. Interesting, impressive, but not very useful.

I finished reading and aligned the papers as McKenzie-Brown looked up.

'A terrible loss,' he said, 'if that's what occurred. I mean . . .'

'Yeah. What about school cadets?'

He offered me his cigarettes and lit one when I refused. 'No cadet unit. Parents are mostly of the conservative persuasion, of course.' He smiled, letting me know he wasn't necessarily of the same mind. 'But some of the women are forceful on the committee and there are a few . . . liberals. The idea has come up from time to time but it has always been voted down.'

'How do the students feel?'

'A school isn't a democracy, Mr Hardy, as you no doubt are aware. But I did make a note from one of the school magazines that Justin took the affirmative in a debate on the proposition that there should be a cadet unit. Argued the case strongly, apparently, and his team won.'

'Why did you make a note of it?'

He leaned back and blew smoke at the ceiling. 'I'm no psychologist, no detective. I'm just a chalkie turned administrator more or less against his will, but when I looked through the material you've seen, it seemed to me there was something bland and conformist about the boy. As if . . .'

'As if he had no personality of his own?'

'That's perhaps putting it a bit strongly but, yes. I've seen it before in intensely religious types. The strong advocacy for the cadets was the only thing that disturbed the pattern.'

No fool this bloke. I told him I only had two more requests—to find out something about the agricultural science excursion to Bangara on the South Coast and to get an idea of what Justin borrowed from the school library. I held up the Serle book.

'I'm returning this. It's well overdue.'

McKenzie-Brown pushed a button on his intercom. 'Jack Simmons is the ag sci master and Robin Crawford looks after the library. I'll get on to them, find you a room of some kind and send them to you.'

I stood and held out my hand. 'You're being very helpful. Thank you.'

We shook. 'Not the uptight place you expected, eh? It still is in some areas but not here, not over this. Have you got any children, Mr Hardy?'

'No.'

'I have three, two girls and a boy. The thought of one of them just vanishing is too much to bear. I did all I could to help the police, but I must say they didn't make your sort of requests. They didn't ask about the cadets, for example. I feel encouraged. I hope you have more success.'

The librarian was the first to arrive in the room, little more than an alcove, that I had been allotted. He was a bustling, busy type who got straight down to business after I handed him the book.

'Thank you. We knew who had it out of course, but under the circumstances we didn't pursue it. I understand you want to know about Justin Hampshire's borrowing habits?'

'That's right.'

Crawford produced a sheaf of cards from the pocket of his reefer jacket. 'He used the library a lot and never incurred any late fees. The parents pay those at the end of term. He borrowed the usual run of textbooks, a little fiction of the thriller type, but far and away his greatest interest was military history. I think it's safe to say he read almost everything the library holds on the subject. That's not such a lot but it ranges over a fair area.'

'The two world wars, the Boer War, Korea, Vietnam . . . ?'

'Oh yes, and more—Sudan, the Malayan Emergency.'

'Any book in particular, taken out more than once, say?'

'Mmm, yes—Bean's *History*, of course, some volumes of the *Australian Dictionary of Biography*, Clarkson's *World War I in Pictures* and something I wasn't at all familiar with, *Australian Monumental Art* by Brigadier-General Henry Woodhouse. He had it out several times. I took it down to look at just before I came. Self-published, presented to the school. I suppose you can guess what it dealt with.'

'War memorials,' I said.

Jack Simmons looked the part—tall, faded sandy hair, weather-beaten face. Unlike McKenzie-Brown and Crawford, he was tieless; his grey shirt was crumpled and stained under the armpits. He slumped into the chair and looked tired. McKenzie-Brown had told me there was a miniature farm in a corner of the school grounds, and Simmons looked as if he'd been doing something physical there.

He glanced at his watch. 'What?' he said.

'An excursion to Bangara a couple of years ago. Justin Hampshire was in the party.'

Simmons straightened a little in the chair. 'He was, and that was the last I ever saw of him.'

'There was a bit of time left at school before the end of the year.'

'He didn't turn up for his classes.'

'Was that unusual?'

'For him, very. He was an excellent student. Could have gone close to topping the state in my subject.'

'Did you do anything about it?'

Simmons shook his head. 'No. There are a lot of pressing problems at that time of year—kids with real difficulties, anxious parents, school assessments to get ready. I suppose I just thought he'd found a better way to use his time. At HSC level the students have a bit of leeway. I was surprised when his excursion report didn't come in though. But by then . . .' He spread his big, freckled hands. 'He was a missing person.'

'Did the police ask you about him?'

'I didn't speak to any police. Not then, not since. You're the first person to question me on the matter and I don't see—'

'Did you notice any difference in Justin on the way back? How did you travel?'

'In a hired people-mover. Different? I don't know. He was always quiet . . . Come to think of it now, I remember that he didn't get out at the rest stops when most of the boys did. Stretch their legs, toss a ball about. I think he'd done that in the past, but this time he just sat and read. As I say, he was a serious lad and the exams were looming. I didn't think anything of it. Why?'

Simmons wasn't exactly friendly or forthcoming but I had no reason to clam up on him. 'As the registrar must have told you, I'm looking into Justin's disappearance for his father.'

'Belatedly, on his part.'

'You're right. But I think I'm picking up a pattern of odd behaviour in the time leading up to when he took off. What you're saying seems to confirm that.'

'I suppose it does. I don't mean to sound defensive, Mr . . . ?'

'Cliff Hardy.'

'Mr Hardy, but the pattern you're talking about doesn't compare in seriousness to some of the behaviour we see at times of stress—like violence or abusive language. I've even seen examples of mild and not so mild self-harm. That's not for public consumption, by the way.'

'Nothing I do is for public consumption, Mr Simmons. I understand what you're saying. Did the boys have free time while they were down there? I suppose you were looking at a farm or something.'

'Vineyards, actually. Yes, they had the best part of an hour to look around the town. The idea being to see if the agricultural history was reflected in the architecture. It usually is, in one way or another.'

'I see. I've got one more question—is there a war memorial at Bangara?'

His pale, washed-out eyes opened wide in surprise. 'I have no idea.'

I went back to the registrar's area and Belinda gave me the original of Justin's mother's note and a warm smile.

'A terrible thing,' she said.

'Yes. Did you know him?'

'Of course. I know them all, more or less.'

'One thing puzzles me, Mrs . . . ?'

The smile again. 'Belinda.'

'Belinda. I don't hear any mention of friends. Kids at school, they usually pal up, don't they? With one or two others? Did Justin?'

She glanced back at McKenzie-Brown's door, looking troubled. 'I'm not sure I should . . .'

'As I said to the teachers, nothing I learn is for public consumption—ever!'

'Justin was what they call a loner, but I did notice that he spent some time with Pierre Fontaine. He was an exchange student from France.'

'Where is he now, d'you know?'

'I don't know. Please don't ask me any more questions.'

Belinda had reached the end of her string of indiscretion. She swivelled around in her chair and began typing as though she had the manuscript of *War and Peace* to finish before she went home and was only halfway through.

I left the school with a few things to think about. I didn't remember seeing the name Pierre Fontaine among those the police had talked to initially. In fact only a couple of students had been interviewed and they were sports team mates, confirming Belinda's judgement—a loner. I really needed to talk to someone of the relevant generation. I didn't have high hopes of Ronny. Sarah seemed the most potentially useful but I didn't have much optimism there either.

I found a phone and called Angela Pettigrew.

'Have you learned anything?' were her first words.

'I'm getting a fuller picture. I really need to talk to Sarah.'

'To Sarah? Why?'

'I gave a lift to the youngster who was there with her yesterday.'

'Why on earth did you do that?'

'It was raining. Sorry, what I mean, is I'll get information any way I can. He told me about something Justin said to Sarah. I'd like to talk to her about it. And there's another—'

'Wait!'

I hung on to the phone and heard voices loud and soft, near and far, as well as music. Then Ms Pettigrew came back on the line.

'She's taken the day off. Not for the first time. She says she'll talk to you but only in person. Really, I don't know. Is it so important?'

'It could be.'

'Where are you now?'

I told her and she said I should come back to the house. That didn't sound like the best of ideas and I said so. She had the answer.

'The dragon mother will absent herself. She'll be in the garden. It needs work.'

A lot of things around that place needed work but the arrangement sounded okay. I stopped at a liquor store and bought a can of draft Guinness. A chop in every glass. A kilometre short of the house I opened the can, carefully let it foam into a paper cup and drank it down. Ah, the gift of we Irish to the human race.

5

The rain had gone and the steps up to the house had dried out, but the water had caused crumbling in some places and a few of the bricks looked ready to head south. Angela was facing some serious maintenance problems. She opened the door to me, ushered me in without speaking, knocked on Sarah's door as we went past and continued through to the sunroom. She was wearing jeans, rubber boots and a faded denim shirt. She picked up a straw hat and a can of insect repellent from a table near the door to the wooden steps leading down to the garden.

'She smokes. I hope you don't mind.'

'A lot do. The smart ones stop.'

'We live in hope.' A quick smile and she was off.

Sarah came into the sunroom wearing white jeans and a black T-shirt with the face of Cold Chisel's Jimmy Barnes printed on it. She was barefoot but stood several centimetres taller than her mother. The makeup had gone and her long, fair hair was pulled back in a ponytail. She was a good-looking young woman with a generous mouth and big eyes that did not bulge in the slightest.

I met her in the centre of the room and we shook hands.

'Hello,' she smiled. 'I'm sorry about what I said to you the other day. Ronny called and said you'd given him a lift. That was nice of you.'

'It was raining pretty hard and he was sloshing along, but I admit I wanted information from him. That's what I do. Let's sit down, Sarah.'

She sat across the low coffee table from me and looked like the private schoolgirl she was—straight back, knees together. 'I know,' she said. 'Angela told me you're trying to find Just.'

'That's right, working for your father.'

Her 'Mmm,' was sceptical.

'I've seen a record of the interview you had with the police back then. You didn't have much to say.'

'I was a kid, and I didn't know anything.'

'Well, you might have known more than you thought. Justin said something to you about being a soldier of fortune. Ronny told me that.'

'Jesus, that's right. But I didn't remember when I was talking to the policewoman. She wasn't very smart. I don't think she knew what she was doing, really.'

'So what can you tell me about that?'

'Hang on.' She got up, hurried out and came back with a packet of Stuyvesant and a lighter. She offered them, I shook my head and she lit up. It was a bit studied but she was getting the hang of it. She moved the squeaky clean ashtray on the table closer and tapped off the minimal amount of ash produced by one draw, the way they do.

'Just was always on about the army and how the Hampshires had fought in every bloody war under the sun. I used to tease him about it and say how America got beaten in Vietnam and how they burnt villages and raped women and that. It made him angry and that's what I wanted to do. I loved him, but . . .' She smoked, tapped ash. 'You know, brothers and sisters, especially after Dad left and Angela went round the bend. It all got a bit, you know, tense. Anyway, this time I said something like that and he just nodded. Then he swore and reckoned he wanted to do it properly, like a soldier of fortune.'

'Did you know what he meant?'

'Not really. I had some rough idea, from a movie or something. I said what about the army, and he said fuck the army.'

'That's all? He didn't mention a country or a place?'

'No, that was it. I thought it was just him sounding off. I didn't even remember it when that dumb policewoman came along. Did I screw things up?'

'No, I don't think so. There's another thing. At Justin's school I was told that he was friendly with someone named Pierre Fontaine. D'you know anything about him?'

Her eyes opened wide and she dropped the cigarette on the glass-topped table. 'Shit!' She picked it up quickly and stubbed it out half smoked in the ashtray.

'Who told you that?'

'I won't say, just as I won't tell anybody else what you're telling me. Them's the rules.'

'You must tell the person who's paying you.' She wasn't dumb.

'Well, there I use my discretion.'

'Did Ronny say anything about Pierre?'

'I hadn't even heard the name until this morning at the school. Should I talk to Ronny about him?'

She shook her head and the ponytail swung. 'I wouldn't.'

'Who is he? Why were you so surprised to hear the name?'

'I was surprised that anyone would say that Just knew him. That guy, Pierre, was done for drugs. He's the one that supplied Ronny with some hash that got him kicked out of Bryce. Justin hated drugs, he was a real pain in the arse about it.' She tapped her cigarette on the edge of the ashtray and held it up. 'He hated smoking and he didn't drink, ever. I can't believe he had anything to do with Pierre.'

'Did you have anything to do with him, Sarah?'

She stood up and went to the louvre windows to check on her mother. 'Sure, I scored some grass off him a couple of times.'

'I have to talk to him to find out what went on between him and Justin. It might help me to trace your brother, although it's worrying. D'you know where I can find him?'

She sat down. 'Of course I do. He got caught supplying heroin to some kids. He's in gaol.'

I sat back and let that sink in while Sarah smoked and looked less cooperative.

'I can understand why Pierre Fontaine's name didn't come up when you and Justin's friends talked to the police,' I said.

She brushed that off with a wave of the cigarette hand. 'Look, Just didn't really have any friends. And I told you, the cops asked dumb questions. They didn't have a fucking clue what was going on.'

'How long after Justin went missing did Fontaine get caught?'

Sarah finished her cigarette and gave some thought

to her answer. 'If you go to see Pierre you won't tell him I talked about him, will you? I mean, he won't be in gaol forever and he's a bad dude.'

'Did I tell you who told me about Fontaine? No. The same goes for you. Like I won't tell your mother you smoke grass.'

She laughed. 'She knows, she just doesn't want to know she knows. All right, let me think. The police got him about a year ago, so it was about a year after Just . . .'

'Went missing.'

She nodded.

I stood. 'Thanks, Sarah. You've been a big help.'

She stood as well and looked surprised to find herself on her feet, being polite. 'Have I? I haven't heard that said before by anyone around here.'

'Give your mother a break. She's holding in a lot of grief and anger. People like her, conventional people, find all this sort of stuff very confusing.'

'You're not conventional, are you, Mr Hardy?'

'I can't afford to be.'

'And I don't want to be.'

'One more thing—Justin went on a school excursion to Bangara near the end of the year and something there seemed to affect him. Does Bangara mean anything to you?'

'Bangara? Yeah, that's where some fucking Hampshire hero came from. Great-grandfather or something. He got killed in the First World War.'

I thanked her again and asked her to thank her mother. She said she would and I believed her. She didn't exactly escort me out, but she made more or less polite gestures along those lines. I gave her a goodbye nod in the passage and she smiled and raised a hand almost shyly, like a schoolgirl.

I didn't take any notes while talking to Sarah, not wanting to put her off, but I scribbled a few things down back in the car. Things to be done, and in this kind of investigation the more the better. I'd had enough of Pittwater and environs and was glad to be heading back to the city. I played some more Joni Mitchell but I was almost at the Spit Bridge before I realised that thinking about the Hampshire case had blotted out every word and note.

I drove to Rose Bay, parked as close as I could to the apartments where Hampshire was staying and asked for him at the service desk. He was out, but at least he was still staying there. I left a message for him to ring me. Back in my office, I phoned Gunnarson.

'You'll be pleased to hear that the dragon lady regards you as competent.'

'I'm thrilled. Did you get anywhere?'

'I might have, but I'm going to need some help.'

He sighed. 'Why is there never any end to what you blokes want?'

'We never sleep.'

I told him in outline about Pierre Fontaine and his possible place in the scheme of things. He swore and condemned all people who held back information from the police. I sympathised.

'He's in gaol somewhere. I don't know where and I don't know for how long. Be a big help if you could get me in to see him.'

'Is that all? Shit, Hardy, haven't you heard of lawyers, prisoners' rights, civil liberties . . . ?'

'Yeah, and I've heard of missing person case files closed.'

He wasn't going to give in too easily. 'How about Hampshire, the skinflint dad? Are you still in touch?'

I didn't exactly lie. 'Yes, but only by phone. He's cagey.'

'He fucking should be. All right, Hardy, leave it with me and I'll get back to you. It could take a while to set up. *If* I can do it, and I'm not saying I can, you'll owe me a big favour. Some serious cooperation with any useful developments might help to square it.'

My next stop was the Fisher Library at the university. Sure enough, it held a copy of the Brigadier-General's *Monumental Art of Australia*. They tell me some self-publishers scatter their books like confetti. This one was a professionally produced effort, though, in a nice typeface with a ton of photos. The text was what you'd call reverent. No index, so I had to leaf through. I found the Bangara memorial arch on page 145. A big, ugly structure, it had been unveiled by the mothers of dead soldiers on Empire Day, 24 May 1924. The arch bore the names of 58 dead and 299 returned AIF members.

Things were coming together. Justin Hampshire knew about the arch and that his great-grandfather's name should be on it. He got his chance to look at it and his behaviour changed after that. Then he went to Canberra to look at the war memorial there. 'Fuck the army', he'd said subsequently. It wasn't too hard to figure out, but I needed confirmation. I felt sure I could find out from some official about the names on the Canberra memorial, but I didn't know a soul in Bangara. Gunnarson had said it'd take time to set up a meeting with the Frenchman. Hampshire had said he had investments; I'd find out tomorrow whether his cheque had cleared. If it had, I'd go to Bangara where Justin Hampshire had learned something that had changed him. I needed to know what it was. Perhaps it had drawn him back there. If the cheque hadn't cleared I still wanted to know, but I'd give serious thought to dobbing Hampshire in for his child support arrears.

6

'What you like about your crappy so-called profession is being able to piss off whenever it suits you.'

That was my ex-wife Cyn's assessment of my attraction to my job and I couldn't say that she was entirely wrong. There were other things—the interesting characters, the edginess, the satisfaction of bringing something to a conclusion—but they wouldn't have cut any ice with Cyn even if I'd spoken about them. A lot of the time we weren't on speaking terms. An architect, she'd blotted me out with cigarette smoke and scale drawings. Well, she had her North Shore stay-at-home advertising executive now, and her two kids, and I could still piss off.

In the morning I pulled out one of my collection of tattered road maps and plotted the route. Hadn't been down that way in years. It was a long run but what the hell. With luck I'd get in a swim and a bodysurf. I filled the Falcon's tank, checked the oil and water and cleaned the windscreen and the back window that had gathered dust on the way back from Pittwater. I also put air in the tyres and the spare. Never let it be said that Hardy went unprepared. But the Smith & Wesson .38 stayed in the house.

It wasn't that kind of a trip, or at least I hoped not.

The weather was warm but the sky was iffy, with dark clouds building and then dissipating as the wind shifted around. I packed my usual summer travelling gear—a change of shirt and socks, a linen jacket, toiletries and shaving stuff, a towel, swimmers and thongs. Robert Hughes for company at night, unless something else turned up. I had a clutch of cassettes taken from the shelf at random, and a camera.

Even bypassing Wollongong on the freeway, it was a slow run through Kiama and Nowra. There was enough of the summer left over for holiday-makers and home-goers to still be using the highway. The traffic thinned out after Ulladulla, and the sky cleared as a strong easterly pushed the threatening clouds inland. I made Bangara by midafternoon and booked into yet another motel. What was the title of that Frank Zappa album—*200 Motels?* Tell me about it.

The memorial was easy to find. It formed the entrance to a large park a block back from the beach. The names of the serving soldiers were on the side away from the water, protecting them from the effects of salty winds and leaving them fairly well preserved after sixty-plus years. Graffitists and vandals had done a certain amount of damage to the edifice but not to the lists of names. Even the antisocial seem to have some respect for names etched in stone. It didn't take long for me to find what Justin had found—the name Hampshire did not appear among the fallen or the returned. I took a couple of photographs.

I was a bit tired after the drive so I sat on a bench in the park under the shade of a tree I couldn't identify and thought about this discovery, or non-discovery. The boy had been brought up to venerate a fallen hero antecedent and found he'd been sold a lie. Given what I'd learned about how locked in to the military traditions he'd been, I could imagine the impact on him. But why didn't he say anything about it to anyone—his sister, his mother, his absent father? Shame perhaps, or anger?

The wind gusted and leaves gathered around my feet and at the base of the arch. The sky clouded over. I wondered whether Justin had sat here before rejoining his party and remaining strangely silent on the return trip, so that even Simmons, not the most sensitive observer, had noticed it.

Bangara had the best south coast features—an estuary formed by Wilson's Creek, a back beach and a surf beach. The town swells in the holiday period and settles back into sleepiness for the rest of the year. Keen surfers come for the waves at off-season times and there is a certain amount of game fishing for those who can't afford the prices further south at Bermagui, where Zane Grey fished in the 30s and Lee Marvin did more recently. I cherished the memory of a photo of Marvin, with his trademark grin, carrying a crate of Great Western champagne down to the boat. The only way to fish.

I strolled along the foreshore and one look cured me of a wish to surf. Under the onshore wind the waves were rolling in as if they intended to build one upon another, collapse and wipe out the beach. Of course they didn't, but they'd throw a bodysurfer around like a cork and there was no fun in that. A swim from the sandy banks of Wilson's Creek looked like the best bet. The surf club building was the usual sturdy bricks and mortar, glass and aluminium structure with cement surrounds. I had Paul Hampshire's photograph of his missing son in my shirt pocket and thought I'd try it on the surfing community. A way to check whether Justin had returned to the scene of his epiphany—a long shot.

Half a dozen people were hanging around the club, four men and two women. They were waxing down boards, smoking, chatting and looking disgruntled at the state of the water. I approached with the photograph and my credentials. Surfers who can't surf get bored easily and my arrival at least provided them with some interest. They were in their twenties, with one of the women, wearing a lifesaver's cap and badge on her swimsuit, looking slightly older than the rest. I sympathised about the waves and told them my business, showing the photograph.

'Surfer, was he?' one of the men asked.

'Yeah, good one apparently.'

'Haven't seen him around here.'

The others looked at the photograph and shook their heads.

'Wouldn't mind, though,' one of the women said.

The older one, the lifesaver, called her a slut in a good-natured way. The first man I'd dealt with seemed reluctant to leave it at that and asked for the name. I told him and one of the others spoke up.

'There's a few of them in the graveyard. I do some gardening up there part-time and I've seen the headstones. Don't know of any around by that name now, but.'

I asked for directions to the graveyard and was told it was across from the park. Perhaps Justin had spent a little more time looking around after all. I thanked them and drove about until I found the entrance. The graveyard was shielded by a long stand of tall trees that were now casting deep shadows across the headstones. A sign said it closed at sunset. I had about an hour.

Country graveyards tend to be overgrown, but this one was reasonably well cared for, with the grass kept under control and the iron railings showing signs of maintenance. Like the memorial arch, the place was partially protected from the salt-laden winds, but time had taken its toll of the inscriptions. Wandering in graveyards isn't my favourite occupation but it has a certain interest. Poignant messages catch your eye, with lives tragically abbreviated by disease and drowning, intermingled with encouragingly long ones. As always, the women lived longer than the men.

I found several Hampshires, husbands and wives and children, but they all dated back to the nineteenth century or the early twentieth at the latest. I took a few photographs for no good reason other than to show Paul Hampshire I'd been on the job. He just might be interested, although it was the absence of an inscription on the memorial that should really interest him.

A longish day, kilometres covered and things learned. Call it satisfactory. I went back to the motel, showered and walked into the township to find somewhere to eat. Choices were few, and a bistro attached to the pub seemed the best bet. I ordered a steak and salad, bought a small carafe of red and settled down in a sheltered part of the beer garden to get mellow. The first glass went down slowly and well and I poured another.

'Hello.'

I looked up from the pouring to see the woman from the surf club—the slightly older lifesaver. She was carrying a tray with my steak, a napkin, cutlery and salt and pepper shakers on it. I half rose, the way you do, and helped her lay out the fixings.

'You're supposed to get the cutlery and the napkin yourself but I made an exception in your case.'

I raised my glass. 'Thanks. Why?'

'I'm a Hampshire,' she said, 'but I'm from a bit of the family that changed its name quite a while back. We're Petersens now—that's with three e's—but my great-grandad was a Hampshire.'

'My name's Cliff Hardy. I'd like to talk to you. You are . . . ?'

She pointed to my plate. 'Better eat while it's hot. I'm Kathy Petersen. Gotta get back to work.'

'When you finish?'

'Sure, why not. Kitchen closes at nine thirty.'

She walked off with her tray. She was tall and lean, sharp-featured, with a confident style. She wore loose trousers and sneakers and a knee-length blue smock with white piping. Her dark hair was cut short. Studs in both ears; no rings.

The steak was fair, the chips good and the salad very good—gave it seven out of ten overall. It was just after eight o'clock so I had time to kill. I ate slowly and went very quietly with the wine. I knew I was no oil painting, with grey creeping into my hair, an obviously broken nose and faint scar tissue over the eyebrows from my boxing days. I hadn't shaved since early morning and the stubble wasn't the careful designer kind, it was just stubble. But she'd seemed interested.

As I'd hoped she would, she came back to collect plates from the few other diners and got to me last.

'How was it?'

'Pretty good.'

'The pub stays open till eleven. I'll meet you in the lounge bar.'

'Right. What do you drink, Kathy?'

She laughed. 'Guess.'

'Brandy and coke.'

'Not bad. Brandy and dry.'

I had her drink ready, and a scotch and soda for me, when she arrived. She'd changed into low heels and wore a red blouse that suited her colouring.

'Well, a detective, eh? Thanks for the drink, I need it after a shift, even though we're not busy.'

We lifted our glasses. 'So you save lives and serve food. Pretty useful.'

She laughed. 'And do relief teaching.'

'Also useful.'

'And you find missing people.'

'Sometimes. Having trouble with this one because it's a couple of years old.'

Without going into too much detail, I told her a bit about the Hampshire case and its difficulties. She listened as she drank, not quickly, not slowly.

'You'll find a couple of Petersens on that arch from World War II and Korea,' she said. 'Great-uncles of mine and a cousin, I think.'

'Do you know why your family name was changed? Or who did it?'

'I knew you were going to ask that. Afraid I don't. It was a few generations ago, as I said. Some sort of family scandal,

I seem to remember, but I don't have the details.'

'Around the time of the First World War, was it? I'll get us another drink while you think about it.'

When I got back with the drinks she shook her head. 'Sorry, not a clue. But I could ask my granny. She's still got her marbles and she might know.'

'If it was a fair dinkum scandal she might not be willing to say.'

'I'm her favourite. I can get around her. She's in a nursing home in Bega, though. It'll take me a few days to get to her.'

'I'd be grateful.' I slapped my pockets. 'I haven't got my cards on me.'

'Where are they?'

'At the motel. Feel like a walk?'

She swilled the rest of her drink. 'Are you married?'

'No.'

'Girlfriend?'

'Not just now.'

'Gay?'

'What do you think?'

'I think I'd like to go back there with you and see what happens.'

She went to the toilet and then we walked the kilometre or so to the motel. The night was mild and the walk was companionable. She wasn't that much shorter than me and when I put my arm around her to steady her over some rough ground, she touched my hand and we locked fingers. We kissed as soon as we got inside and it went on from there—a bit hectic but experienced, not uncontrolled.

Her body was tanned and firm and she liked to be touched. I wasn't exactly sex-starved but it had been a while and I was aroused and eager. She fished a condom from her blouse on the floor and rolled it on to me. We left the bedside lights burning and didn't turn them off until much later.

7

I'd ordered the standard motel breakfast—sausages, bacon, eggs and tomato with soggy toast and thin coffee—for six thirty, and we shared it. Kathy said she had to be back near her phone by eight in case she was called on to teach.

'You'll be heading back to the smoke,' she said.

'That's right.'

'So, a one-night stand.'

She was clear-eyed and the absence of the little make-up she'd had on the night before didn't make any difference. She'd put her hair in order with her fingers. A change of clothes and she'd be classroom-ready. I got a card from my wallet and put it in front of her.

'Try to find some time to come up,' I said. 'How about Easter?'

'Mmm, maybe.'

'Or when I get this done I could come down for a bit, if you . . .'

'Don't get me wrong. I don't feel guilty about a one-night stand. I don't need consoling.'

'I'm not consoling you. I'm trying to give myself something to look forward to.'

'I suspect you're bad news for women, Cliff. Not that you mean to be, just the way things work out with you.'

She was more right than wrong but I didn't want that to be the whole story, not after the pleasure we'd shared. 'We barely know a thing about each other, Kathy. Why don't you ring me after you talk to your grandmother, whether you find out anything or not. We can talk. As you said, see what happens.'

She'd been wearing her bra and panties with her blouse unbuttoned. She came around the table and kissed me and she had that lovemaking smell that would have got me going again except that she was buttoning up and reaching for her pants.

'It's a deal,' she said.

'I'll drive you.'

She shook her head. 'It's no distance. I'll walk and try not to feel too encouraged. Talk to you soon, Cliff.'

She slid into her trousers, pulled on her shoes, scooped up her bag and pantyhose and left.

I went up the coast road to Bateman's Bay and over the mountain to Canberra. The Falcon ticked a bit on the climb but it does that to show it needs mechanical attention from time to time. I was in a good mood after the time with Kathy and the prospect of more of the same, and the feeling that I was making some kind of progress with the case.

Like a lot of people, I felt ambivalent about Canberra. It was a good idea to put it where it is as a counterweight to Sydney and Melbourne. Because of the concentration of intelligent, well-educated people, it behaves progressively at the ballot box, unlike the rest of the country most of the time. But the neatness of the layout, the manicured gardens, the sense of being so planned made me wonder if it'd ever feel like a city. Good place to study, make a career, but to live? I wasn't so sure of that.

As monuments to human folly go, the Canberra war memorial wasn't so bad, tasteful even. The triumphalism is kept more or less in check, and it feels like a place for reflection rather than celebration, at least in spots. Passing the shell of the miniature Japanese submarine scooped out of Sydney Harbour, I spared a thought for those small young men who'd taken on what was virtually a suicide mission. I tossed some coins into the water in recognition of all the other poor bastards who'd gone through the meat grinder. The honour roll does the job it's supposed to do without too much fuss.

As I traced the names, I imagined Justin Hampshire here more than two years ago. His Honda in the car park, the money from the sale of his sporting gear running low and his dreams in tatters. The Bangara memorial arch record was confirmed. There were no fallen Hampshires at Gallipoli or the Somme or anywhere else in the war to end all wars. And none in World War II or Korea. As Kathy had said, there were two Petersens, with the distinctive spelling of the name she had made a point of, killed in the Western Desert, no doubt fighting against Rommel, the Desert Fox, and one in Korea. The John Prine lyric about losing Davey in the Korean War and the father still not knowing what for, came to mind. Justin's family had a military tradition all right, but with the name change it wasn't one he'd had any way of knowing about.

You're supposed to feel sad in such places. I did—for all the waste, and for Justin.

No reason to hang around. I didn't think I was likely to bump into Hawkie or Keating to advise them about what to do for the good of the country. The drive from Canberra to Sydney was forgettable. About the only thing of interest was the low level of water in Lake George. Cattle were grazing in places where once they would have had to swim.

Back in Sydney I used an ATM and found that Hampshire's cheque had cleared. Encouraging. I drove to Rose Bay and parked, semi-legally, within walking distance of the apartments where Hampshire was staying. I asked for him at the desk and was told he was in. The receptionist buzzed him but got no answer. I took the lift to the third floor and knocked. No response.

I raised my voice. 'Mr Hampshire, it's Cliff Hardy. They tell me downstairs you're in so please open the door. You're a hard man to catch up with.'

The door opened and Hampshire stood there, leaning against the jamb for support. He was unshaven, in a singlet and trousers, barefoot. His eyes were bloodshot and he smelled of liquor and vomit. There were stains on his singlet and pants.

'Hello, Hardy.' His voice was slurred and he wasn't looking at me.

'Hello yourself.' I pushed past him and went into the flat. The serviced apartment needed servicing. It was a mess, with clothes, newspapers, bottles and fast food containers spread around. A sheet of paper by the telephone was covered with numbers and scribble. Hampshire stumbled after me.

'Sorry about the mess.'

'You're a bigger mess. What the fuck's happened to you?'

He slumped into a chair. 'Have you got a cigarette?' He pronounced it the American way with the accent on the first syllable. 'I'm out.'

'No. What's got you into this state?'

He rubbed his stubble. No natty bow tie now, no spiffy handkerchief. I saw what it was about the hair now; he wore a toupee, a bit bedraggled.

'You know I said I had investments, interests in things? Well, I've been screwed by an accountant and a lawyer. I'm going to have to figure out a way to take legal action against them. I guess I panicked a bit.' He waved at the mess. 'But I'll get it together. Now, have you made any progress?'

'Why don't you get cleaned up and tidy this joint a little. Then I'll feel more confident about talking to you.'

'Who the hell do you think you are?'

'I know who I am. I'm not sure who you are or what you're worth.'

He seemed about to bluster but stopped himself and looked down at the stains on his singlet. 'You're right. I have to get a grip. Give me a few minutes.'

He went away and I heard the shower running. I did some of the tidying myself—dumping the food containers in the kitchen bin, emptying the ashtrays, collecting the bottles and making a stack of the newspapers. Several of the papers were open at the business pages, showing the stock market with some stocks underlined. None I'd ever heard of. From the look of the notepad he'd made dozens of phone calls. A lot of the numbers were covered with scribble, some had crosses beside them; a couple had ticks countermanded by crosses.

I was deliberately holding the notepad when he came back. It was a test. He was shaved and his hair was slicked back. He had on a clean shirt and trousers and wore shoes. He didn't protest about my snooping.

'Tell me about Justin.'

I brought him up to date on what I'd discovered and each piece of information seemed to hit him like a brick.

'My grandmother told me my grandfather was killed in France.'

'You didn't think to check?'

'No. I accepted it. I was . . . proud of it. God help me. I only wished it had been at Gallipoli so that—'

'You could worship all the harder?'

He nodded.

'What about your father?'

'My mother said he was killed in New Guinea.'

'Kokoda?'

'She wasn't specific, but that was . . . the impression she gave me.'

'And you passed it on to Justin.'

He nodded. 'You say he found out it wasn't true in either case?'

'Yes. Bright kid. And your wife spilled the beans on your less than glorious Vietnam record after you shot through.'

'Jesus.'

'I suppose you amped that up a bit.'

'Yes.'

'One way and another, you helped to produce a very angry, disappointed and disillusioned young man. It's no wonder he took off.'

He moaned, but whether for himself or Justin it was hard to tell. 'I'm sorry. I had no idea. But where did he go? What did he do?'

I opened my hands. 'That's why you hired me, but it's getting complicated and in more ways than you know.'

'What do you mean?'

I told him about Justin's apparent association with a man now serving prison time for drug offences. He shook his head as if unable to take the information in.

'Why would he have anything to do with a drug pusher?'

'I'm trying to get to see the guy. I might find out or I might not, but you have to get yourself ready for bad news.'

'Not knowing is just constant bad news. I've got some stocks I can sell. That won't get me out of all of the holes I'm in but I'll raise enough to be able to keep paying you. I want you to see this through right to the end, whatever it is.'

I nodded. 'Sorry, but I've got one more kick in the guts for you. Angela's dobbed you in to the welfare people for not paying child support. They'll refer it to the cops who'll be on the lookout for you. I've gone out on a bit of a limb there, told the cop I'm in contact with that I didn't know where you were.'

'Why did you do that?'

I shrugged. 'You're paying me, for one thing.'

'From what I've heard of you there must be more to it than that.'

He'd touched on something that Cyn had never understood—the sheer interest a case like this set up, the way it got under my skin, into my head and needed to be resolved. But it wasn't something I wanted to talk about. I took out my notebook and consulted it, just to have something to do, to let that thought drift away. 'I haven't heard your side of the story,' I said. 'In my experience there usually is one. Did you pay child support?'

'Not always . . . when I could. But I paid Sarah's and Justin's school fees all the way and I signed the house over to Angela. There's very little mortgage on it and Angela has some money of her own. Is she . . . all right?'

'Yes and no. Sarah's a problem and the place looks a bit rundown. But I'd say she's pretty tough. Losing you and Justin rocked her, but I suppose she thinks she's fighting back. She is, in a way. She was helpful to me and now she's trying to get back at you. I know you went to the States on business. Why did you stay?'

He grimaced. 'I fell in love, or thought I did. I wish I hadn't. Some client you've got, Hardy.'

'I've had worse,' I said. 'One came at me with an axe. Got anything left to drink?'

8

I had a couple of weak scotch and waters with Hampshire, partly because I was ready for a drink and partly to see how he was handling his liquor after an apparent binge. Seemed all right. I advised him to move in case the authorities got onto any of the people he'd contacted to trace him. He said he would and that he'd get in touch with me as soon as he had. I told him his retainer would hold me on the job for a while and he repeated his promise to keep me in funds to the end.

I walked around Rose Bay for a while, for the exercise and to allow the blood alcohol level to drop. A lot of the big old houses had been converted into flats but not all. There was a lot of money here in bricks and mortar and, as up at Pittwater, in boats. I speculated about what the land occupied by the Royal Sydney Golf Course was worth—too much to calculate. Cyn's father had been a member and he'd told me the yearly dues which, at the time, amounted to something like half of my annual income. It was probably much the same now.

I went home and dealt with the mail and the phone messages—nothing that couldn't wait. It was getting on towards that time when I had to decide whether to scramble eggs or go out to eat or just buy some takeaway. A constant question. Sometimes I thought that the solution in the sci-fi books or for the astronauts—a pill containing all the necessary nutrients—would be the solution. But they never seemed to wash it down with a good red or white.

Gunnarson rang while I was mulling it over. He told me he'd arranged for me to see Pierre Fontaine the day after next.

'He can see anyone he wants to.'

'Why's that?'

'He's in a hospice in Woolloomooloo. He's dying of AIDS, they reckon.'

I went up Glebe Point Road to my favourite Italian and had lasagne and a salad and a couple of belts of the house chianti and a long black. It was raining when I left and I got soaked on the way back. I didn't care—it seemed like a fitting sealer to a strange day that had started out well with Kathy and taken some strange twists and turns after that. Not that unusual. I dumped almost everything I'd been wearing for the past two days in the washing machine and set it running. I went to bed to read about the convicts and their masters, who'd probably built some of the houses at Rose Bay.

I was showered but not shaved, wearing a threadbare terry towelling dressing gown I was fond of, buttering my toast, coffee in the mug, when a hammering came on the door and the bell rang. Toast in hand, I went to answer it. About the only people I know of who wear ties with business shirts and black leather jackets are cops.

'Mr Hardy?'

I nodded. He showed his warrant card. 'Detective Sergeant Ian Watson, Northern Command. I have to ask you some questions.'

'I hope I have the answers. Come on in.' I said this quickly and turned away so that he had a choice—follow me in or call me back. His response would give me an idea of the seriousness of whatever was going on. I assumed it was to do with my shielding of Paul Hampshire. Serious, but not too serious.

'Please come back, Mr Hardy. I don't want to enter your home.'

Uh-oh, serious then. I came back—but Hardy's rule is never give an inch.

'House, Sergeant,' I said. 'Around here we have houses. Homes are on the North Shore and in the eastern suburbs.'

He was about my size and age and holding together pretty well except that, like me, he showed signs of facial damage and some professional hard yards. He put his card away and gave me a look that told me my jibe hadn't touched him.

'I was told you were difficult. Right. I'll see you in the detectives' room at the Glebe station in half an hour. If you're not there I'll show you how difficult I can be.'

'What's it about?'

But he'd turned away and was already at the gate. He hadn't stumbled over the lifting tiles on the porch or the sagging cement blocks on the path. He left the gate open. I judged he'd won the first round on points.

I ate the toast, drank some coffee, shaved and turned on Radio National to get the weather. It was going to be warm and stay that way until a late cool change. I put on drill trousers, battered Italian loafers and a denim shirt worn to a comfortable thinness. Clothes maketh the man—relaxed, innocent. But I phoned Viv Garner, my solicitor, who lived in Lilyfield and spent very little time in his office, and asked him to stand by in case I needed him.

'What now?' Viv said.

'I don't know, I honestly don't know.'

I've been in the Glebe police station more times than I can count and much more often than I wanted to. I can only remember one time when it did me any good—when my car was stolen and the police got it back. Otherwise, it was an exercise in mutual distrust and antagonism. I walked there, presented myself more or less on time, and was taken upstairs to the detectives' room. It smelled of cigarette smoke, hamburgers and take-out coffee. The Glebe boys had cleared a desk for Watson in a corner, giving him something like semi-privacy.

I sat down while he flicked through a notepad. Then he shook a card out of a paper evidence bag and let it fall right-side-up on the desk between us.

'This is yours,' he said.

I had to turn my head a little. 'Yes.'

He used a pen to slide it across the surface and back into the bag. 'When did you last see Angela Pettigrew?'

I shook my head. 'No, Sergeant, I'm not going to come at that. You tell me why I'm here, why you have my card in an evidence bag, or I walk out and phone my solicitor.'

'Worth a try,' he said, and nodded to one of the Glebe detectives who'd been watching with some amusement. 'Angela Pettigrew was murdered some time yesterday.'

No matter how or when or how often it happens, learning that someone you know has died makes an impact. I leaned back in the chair and took in a deep breath of the smelly air.

'How?'

'I don't think we'll go into that. You left your card for her. We need to know when you saw her and why.'

'I actually left the card for her daughter. But I saw her the day before yesterday. I was hired to locate her son, who's been missing for over two years.'

'Hired by her?'

'No.'

'Don't piss me off, Hardy. Hired by who?'

'Whom.'

He let that go by. 'What was her state of mind when you saw her?'

'She had a failed marriage, a missing son and a difficult daughter. She wasn't a happy woman. And if you want to see my notes on the interview you can forget it.'

For all his tough exterior and aggressive style, Watson wasn't going to make life harder for himself than it needed to be.

'Okay,' he said. 'You don't like me and I don't like you. Neither of us likes being here or talking about a woman being killed. Can we cut the shit and try to do something useful?'

So I told him about the Hampshire–Pettigrew problem and about my confrontation with Ronny and the later conversation and my meeting with Sarah. In line with him not revealing anything about how Angela was killed, I was selective. Watson scribbled notes in shorthand. Useful talent.

'Ronny who?'

'I don't know. Wasn't told.'

'He hit Ms Pettigrew?'

I peered at his notes. 'I hope you've got the squiggle right. I said he *pushed* her. I did the hitting.'

'Of a juvenile.'

'As big as me or you, and faster if he got a chance, I'd reckon. Now, let's have a bit from you. How was Ms Pettigrew killed?'

He paused, but I'd said enough to convince him I wasn't at Church Point the day before. He wanted more from me though, so he decided to play along: 'She was beaten to death with a ceramic ornament.'

'No chance of an accident—a blow and a fall?'

'None. Where's the ex-husband?'

I gave him the address in Rose Bay, hoping that Hampshire had moved as I'd advised. I didn't think it likely that he'd killed Angela. All the indications were that he'd spent the time drinking and smoking while trying to get his financial affairs in order, as he'd said. Still, you never know. In any case, it'd be better for him if he contacted the police rather than have them hunt him down. I figured it was my turn for a question.

'Where's the daughter, Sarah?'

'She's there. Distressed. She found the body. A policewoman's with her and a neighbour.' He consulted his notes, 'You haven't really said anything about the missing son. D'you reckon he'll turn up?'

I shrugged. I'd been about as cooperative as he could have expected, but he still didn't like me and he decided to let it show.

'Oh, maybe I haven't asked the right question. Do you think you can find him? Or *have* you found him?'

'All that's between me and my client.'

'I suppose this is the fiftieth fucking time you've been told you have no privilege.'

'Being a shitkicking private nuisance? Yeah, about that often.'

He closed the notebook. 'I think that's all for now, but if we need to talk again, and we probably will, you'll make yourself available, won't you?'

'Under the right conditions, yes.'

'I don't have to tell you to stay away from the people involved in this, do I?'

'Including my client?'

He didn't answer. He put his card down in front of me, got up and went across to the senior detectives' glassed-in room. The cop who'd been watching us from time to time as he went about his paperwork waved me out.

At the phone booth outside the post office I called the number I had for Hampshire and was told he'd checked out the day before. I went home but there was no message on the answering machine. I drove to Darlinghurst and heard on the radio news about the death of a woman at Church Point which the police were investigating. The light was blinking on the office machine and Hampshire's message told me he was at another set of serviced apartments, this time in Crows Nest. I rang and got him.

'Hardy, what's up?'

'I've got some bad news for you.'

'Justin, is he . . . ?'

'No, it's Angela. I'm sorry to have to tell you. She's dead. She's been murdered. The police came to me because I left my card in the house.'

'My God.'

'Yeah, it's very bad. Are you in control now, not fucked up like yesterday?'

'You don't think I . . . ?'

'You have to contact the police and cooperate with them. They'll find you eventually and it'd be much better for you to do as I say.'

'Angela, she . . .'

'Don't lose your grip. There's your daughter to think of, and maybe, if Justin's around somewhere and he hears, he might surface.'

'D'you really think so?'

'I haven't the faintest fucking idea. Here's the number of the cop who's on the investigation team. Ring him and tell him where you are. He'll have an answering service or a beeper or something. It's going to be tough. You might have to identify her. You'd better be up to it. Have you got a lawyer?'

I heard him suck in a breath as if he was gearing himself up for the ordeal. 'I've got more lawyers hanging off me than I need.'

'Alert one you can rely on.'

'How do I say I heard about Angela?'

It was a funny thing about the Hampshires—him, Angela, Sarah, and Justin as well for all I knew—they were bright enough to see the angles when they were under pressure. Maybe too bright for their own good. And that went with a capacity to put things in compartments, hold things back. We're all like that, I suppose, but these people seemed to make an art form of it.

'Tell them the truth, for Christ's sake. I gave them your previous number. You moved and told me the new one. I told you about Angela and now you're doing everything you can to help. Lie, and they'll make things even harder for you.'

'Thanks, Hardy.'

'For what?'

'For believing in me.'

'I didn't say that.'

I rang off and left him to it. I didn't make the point that Sarah would be his responsibility from now on. He had enough to worry about. I had to hope that the police didn't find any evidence against him sufficient to hold him for more than the regulation time. Eventually I'd need more money if I was going to keep looking for Justin and the case had me completely hooked by now. I couldn't see a connection between Angela's death and my search, but I had to consider it.

9

I had nothing to do but wait. I was due to see Pierre Fontaine at the hospice the next morning. More flak would be coming from the police, especially if they didn't latch on to Ronny. I rang Viv Garner again and told him the cops hadn't locked me up yet because I hadn't done anything I shouldn't.

'I'll take that with a sack of salt, Cliff,' he said. 'But call if you need me.'

There was nothing in the office that required urgent attention but I filled in the time doing non-urgent things like putting a new ribbon in the typewriter. I listened to the news and got a repeat of the item about the woman killed at Church Point. No name, no developments. The next item was about the government's idea for an identity card to be called the Australia Card. It'd have all the information on it you needed to get things you needed and all the information they needed to get you. I was against it, although I knew almost everything was on file about almost everyone somewhere.

I remembered a friend named Jim telling me about the difficulty he had registering the name and details of his second illegitimate child. The Canberra official said illegitimate children couldn't have siblings, not officially.

'She's got the same mother and father,' Jim said.

'Why don't you just marry the woman and everything would be straightforward.'

Jim, a big bloke with a ready wit but a short fuse said, 'Because I don't want to make it easy for bastards like you.'

I felt pretty much that way about the Australia Card.

That memory made me smile, the first bit of amusement since I'd been with Kathy Petersen. The phone rang. I wasn't in the mood for more work or free to do it, so I let the machine take the call. It was her.

'Hello, Cliff, just checking to see if you—'

I picked up. 'Kathy.'

'I was going to say, to see if you spent any time in your office or were always on the prowl.'

'As little as possible. Good to hear you. No teaching, no surf?'

'No teaching and that bloody south-westerly's still blowing. Do you surf?'

'Used to. Not for a while. The boards have changed, not sure how good I'd be.'

'Were you good?'

'Fair.'

'How's your investigation going?'

I realised that it had been a long time since I'd had anyone to talk to about what I did, even in general terms. No partner for a few years, the last tenant in my house had moved out long ago and my best friend, Frank Parker, being a senior cop and recently appointed Deputy Commissioner, didn't want to engage in what was virtually shoptalk. We talked sport mainly, and I talked writs with

Viv Garner and sprains and contusions with my doctor mate, Ian Sangster.

'It's getting complicated. Did you hear about the woman killed at Church Point?'

'Yes.'

'She was the mother of my missing kid.'

'Jesus, that's nasty. Is it connected with what you're doing?'

'I don't see how but it means I'm going to have cops checking me over for a bit. Not that that's anything new. I told them where I was yesterday, had to. Didn't mention you, but you might confirm that I ate dinner in the pub.'

She laughed. 'Sorry, it's no laughing matter. I'll confirm that you stayed the night if they ask. I've got nothing to hide and . . . I enjoyed it.'

'So did I.'

A slight pause, then she said, 'Well, I've got things to do. I wanted to tell you I'm going to Bega to talk to Grandma tomorrow. I'll let you know if I learn anything useful.'

'Call me anyway. This'll sort out one way or another, so try and keep Easter free. Can I have your number?'

She rattled it off. 'Don't feel obligated,' she said. 'Sounds as if you've got enough on your plate. See you, Cliff.'

The mail brought bills and with Hampshire's retainer in the account I wrote out a few cheques and, thinking about lunch, went down to post them in the box at the quiet section of Forbes Street. I dropped the envelopes in the box and felt a hard punch to the right kidney that drove the wind out of me. I spun around, fighting for breath, and took a solid thump down where you don't want it. The toast and coffee threatened to come up, my eyes flooded and closed against the pain and I sagged against the postbox, still gasping, and with no strength to retaliate.

'Keep your mouth shut, Hardy. If you chuck over me I'll really hurt you.'

I knew the voice and as my vision cleared I recognised the face. Billy 'Sharkey' Finn had been briefly middleweight champion of Australia five years ago before the booze and drugs got to him. He lost the title and a few more bouts, some certainly thrown for a payoff from the gamblers, and became a standover man for various heavy Sydney crims. Sharkey was fat now, a heavyweight for sure, but he was still strong. In my struggling condition he had no trouble half dragging, half carrying me to a car that drew up nearby. He held me up with one hand, opened the door and shoved me into the back seat.

The man sitting there was impeccably dressed in a lightweight suit and he was barbered and manicured to within an inch of his life—Wilson Stafford, a 'colourful racing identity' to the tabloids. We'd crossed paths once years back. Stafford used to do some of his own muscle work then. I'd helped a pub owner keep Stafford's rigged pokies out of his Summer Hill hotel. The car was a Daimler with leather seats and a bar and telephone. Stafford smiled at me with his perfectly capped teeth.

'We meet again.'

I was still sucking in air as Sharkey flopped into the front passenger seat.

'If that fat tank artist wants to come at me from the front,' I said, 'I'll make him uglier than he already is.'

'You hear that, Sharkey?' Stafford said.

'I heard. Any time, Hardy. Any time.'

Stafford took a cigarette from a gold case and lit it with a gold lighter. He adjusted the cuffs on his shirt, showing me the solid gold monogrammed links. 'I'd like to see it. But not now. I took the opportunity to pay you back for the trouble you caused me, Hardy. But we've got other business today.'

'What would that be?'

'That cunt Paul Hampshire's back. Bald bastard's wearing a fuckin' wig. And you've seen him. One of my people spotted you and that heap of shit you drive in Rose Bay where Hampshire was staying.'

'So?'

'So the dumb prick was slow getting the information to me and the cunt's not there now and I want to know where he is.'

'Why?'

'Why d'you fuckin' think? He owes me money.'

'I get the impression he owes money to quite a few people.'

'Not like he does with me. He ripped me off big time and then shot through to America.'

'That's interesting.'

'Don't be smart with me unless you want more of what you just had.'

'I'd be ready for him now and I'd make it a bit harder. Your driver doesn't look like much and you're well past it, Wilson.'

Finn half turned and showed the business end of a pistol, silencer fitted.

'That's different,' I said. 'But I can't help you. Hampshire's wife was murdered yesterday and right now he's talking to the police—dunno who, dunno where.'

'Fuck,' Stafford said. 'How do you know that?'

'Because he rang me this morning and I told him to get in touch with them. I didn't know he had a problem with you. I wish he'd told me and I'd have been ready for the canvas back kid there.'

'Hardy, you—'

Stafford cut him off. 'Shut up, Sharkey. I have to think about this. I thought he'd hired you as protection.'

'No.'

'Why, then?'

'That's between me and him, but it's got nothing to do with you.'

Stafford smoked his cigarette down to the filter and stubbed it out. It was the lunch hour and there were a few people in the street now. Finn put the gun away. I opened the door.

'If that's all, I'll be going.'

Stafford lit another cigarette. 'You can give Hampshire a message. I—'

I gripped his wrist, shook it and he dropped his lighter. 'Fuck you. You say you held a grudge against me and got even. Well, I've got a grudge against you and Sharkey now and I'll leave you a little something to think about.'

I got out of the car, took my Swiss army knife from a pocket, opened the short blade and slid it quickly into both whitewalled back tyres. Then I joined the people walking towards the steps leading down to William Street. Petty maybe, but satisfying.

*

I bought a salad roll in William Street and went back to the office. I had a drop of red to wash it down and as an aid to thought. I had an old sawn-off shotgun I'd taken from a disgruntled client. There were no shells then or now, but I put it on the desk anyway. Not that I really expected trouble, but with someone barely under control like Sharkey Finn, it pays to be cautious.

I tried to remember exactly what Stafford's reaction had been when I told him about Angela Pettigrew. Had he looked surprised? I couldn't remember, there was too much going on. But now there was plenty to think about. If Hampshire had enemies like Wilson Stafford, he'd pulled a lot of wool over my eyes. He was in serious danger. Did the police know anything about his activities? Watson had played his cards very close to his chest and I felt dumb about being so much in the dark. There were candidates now for Angela's killer and maybe whatever it was Hampshire had done had implications for what had happened to Justin. It wasn't looking good from any angle.

Barry Templeton was a sworn enemy of Wilson Stafford. He was more intelligent than Stafford, marginally less ruthless, and a lot better company. We met occasionally when I played tennis at White City with Frank Parker. Templeton was a good player and it amused him to belong to the same club as a senior police officer. They got along okay in a wary kind of way and the three of us had the odd drink, with Frank being careful not to let Templeton pay for anything. I wasn't so circumspect, but I could see Frank's point, with police corruption always in the news and the media always on the lookout.

Templeton owned a restaurant in Paddington and he was invariably there at night, enjoying the food, keeping an eye on the quality of the service and no doubt doing deals that wouldn't bear a lot of scrutiny. He'd crossed swords with Stafford over shares in a couple of racehorses and they'd never been reconciled.

Rudi's, as Templeton's restaurant was called, was in Oxford Street and was well patronised by people like himself: certain cops and lawyers, journalists, media stars and wannabes. I'd been there a few times, running interference for some hard types who felt in need of a little backup—unnecessarily as it turned out. The food was good, the atmosphere smoky and the wine expensive. The meal was going to put a hole in the money Hampshire had paid me but I wasn't feeling well disposed towards him at that point. I booked a table for one for nine pm; Templeton dined late.

'What name, sir?'

'Cliff Hardy. You might tell Barry I want to have a word with him.'

I went home to shine my shoes, look for a clean shirt and brush down my suit. You have to look your best at Rudi's. I soaked in the bath for a long time to let the hot water ease the pain in my kidney and below the belt. Sharkey was an expert at fouling opponents and he'd got me with two good ones, but they hadn't been as solid as you'd expect from a professional. He was fat and slow and lacking a bit of zip. I pissed and didn't pass blood—Sharkey had lost his touch. I fancied my chances if we met up again on a level playing field. The gun was a worry, though.

I lay in the cooling water and thought about my conversation with Kathy and our earlier encounter. My reaction was encouraging and confirmed that, again, Sharkey hadn't done the damage he might have. I shaved, dressed and treated myself to a solid gin and tonic to clean the pipes, stimulate the appetite and console myself. Going out to eat solo isn't much fun, but with luck the evening would pay dividends. And I remembered that the barramundi at Rudi's was very good.

10

Whoever the original Rudi was, he had constructed an excellent eatery. The restaurant was on two levels with outdoor areas on both as well as pavement dining on the ground floor, weather permitting. The tables weren't too tightly packed and they ran from two-seaters to long set-ups capable of taking up to twenty. I'd specified outside at the back. I knew that was where Templeton usually placed himself, at a table never larger than for four. The chairs were comfortable and the settings unfussy. The piped music was unobjectionable and the waiters and waitresses were brisk and efficient.

I ordered whitebait for starters and the barramundi—always a seafood man when I know it's good. A bottle of riesling, hold the bread. The place was full or close to it, and the ceiling fans were doing a reasonable job. I draped my jacket over the back of my chair and sipped some water.

'Cliff, mate, good to see you.'

One of those moments—I knew him but didn't know his name. I shook his hand and forced a smile.

'Bryan Harvey, you remember me—from the Amplex business.' He was still holding my hand and I shook it again enthusiastically as it all came back to me. Harvey was a Glebeite who'd fought long and hard against a developer's plan to build units right down to the water on a site left toxic through years of occupation by factories. I was in the fight too, attending meetings and onsite demos. I remembered Harvey walking around with his hand cupped satirically behind his back as one of the councillors talked up the project.

Harvey was so disgusted he ran for council himself and won. In the end, Amplex had to modify their plan to leave a decent space between the units and the water and contribute to the rehabilitation of an adjacent wetland. He said he was off the council now but still fighting the good fight for the environment. I said I was still in the same game. We told each other how well we looked and he went off to join a party of five at another table. Good bloke.

The wine arrived just before the whitebait, as it should, and the barramundi came along exactly at the right time too. Rudi's prided itself on efficient service of this kind, not easy to achieve in a busy restaurant. I was halfway through the fish when Barry Templeton dropped into the other chair. He'd brought another bottle of the same wine with him and a glass which he filled after topping up mine.

'Nice to see you, Cliff. Bit sad to see you dining alone but then, I know you're here on business.'

I raised my glass. 'That's right, Barry. I see business is booming. This arm of it anyway.'

'All arms, my friend, all arms. Now, it'd be nice to chat and I'm glad to see you're enjoying the fish, but I've got things to attend to, so what's on your mind?'

Templeton was a smoother customer than Stafford. Equally well turned out but he wore his clothes with a more relaxed air, didn't need to fiddle with his tie and cuffs. I told him I'd had a run-in with Stafford and about my connection with Paul Hampshire. The mention of the name brought a smile to Templeton's face.

'Ah, yes,' he said, taking a sip of the wine. 'Mr Under-the-radar himself.'

I dug into the remains of the fish. 'Meaning?'

'Tell me there's some grief in this for Stafford.'

I packed my fork with the last chunk of fish. 'There might be but I can't promise. I can't see the connection yet between what I'm looking into and the beef between Stafford and Hampshire. It's possible. I can tell you there's some grief for Sharkey Finn if I catch him without a gun in the right place at the right time.'

'I've no time for Sharkey, but Wilson belongs deep down out beyond the Heads, so possible's good enough for me. This is what I know.'

He told me that Paul Hampshire was a conman—a floater of get-rich-quick schemes that went wrong but not before Hampshire had skimmed the cream off the top. 'The thing was,' Templeton said, 'although he cooked the scams up here and picked his targets, the location was always somewhere else—New Zealand, Fiji, the Cook Islands, places like that. He specialised in money laundering for people who had incomes they couldn't account for. A serious problem. He'd launder it until it was pretty well washed away, but always in another jurisdiction. And the targets didn't really have any comeback if they didn't want the tax office up their arses.'

'Sounds bloody dangerous to me,' I said.

'Not really. I'm not talking about heavy criminals here or about big sums of money. Nice little earners for Hampshire though, and he'd always make himself scarce afterwards. Went to America, I believe. I think he's got dual citizenship.'

'What about Stafford?'

Templeton laughed. 'That's where he made his big score. The way I heard it, Stafford came to him through some intermediary looking like the sort of guy Hampshire was used to. This time it was big money Stafford needed to squirrel away. I don't know the details. Some kind of currency fiddle. The result was that Stafford lost the dough and Hampshire took off. Somehow it must have dawned on him that Stafford was a different kind of . . . client, so he stayed away. You say Hampshire's back, eh?'

'Did I say that?'

We'd both been working quietly on the wine and the bottle I'd ordered was gone. Templeton inspected the other bottle, which was still at a satisfactory level. He poured himself a little more and stood.

'I didn't expect you to tell me anything, Cliff, and it's no skin off my arse. Happy to help make Stafford unhappy, and I know you have a knack of doing that to people.'

'Thank you,' I said.

Templeton smiled. 'I'd like to say the meal's on me, but why the fuck should I? Say hello to Frank and try to improve that backhand. See you, Cliff.'

I cleaned up the last of the baby potatoes in sour cream and the asparagus, cool but still good. I ordered a long black and, since I'd come by taxi and was intending to go back the same way, I had another solid belt of the wine. Thinking back, I should have had suspicions about Hampshire early on. The bow tie, the display hanky, the toupee. The man was an actor and he'd played to his audience. But I needed the work and the problem he'd presented me with was intriguing. It still was, but it was running in all sorts of confusing directions.

The morning radio news had a report on the death in Spain of 'Aussie' Bob Trimboli, a Griffith drug kingpin who was wanted on various charges, including murder. He'd skipped to Spain and pulled the wool over some official eyes. That's when he wasn't greasing their palms. I'd run into him once when I was doing a bit of bodyguarding for a politician who'd had dealings with Trimboli that he'd come to regret. The politician had to confront Trimboli just once more and needed support to do it. The meeting was tense. I disliked them both about equally and I had to hurt one of Trimboli's offsiders to see my man safe. There was no one happier than me when 'Aussie' Bob took off for the Costa Brava.

The bulletin carried a brief follow-up report on the death of a woman at Church Point. So brief as to be almost meaningless—no names, no details—and so bloodless it had all the hallmarks of a tight police clampdown. No invitation to the public to help. The newspaper coverage was much the same.

The Catholic hospice was in Woolloomooloo. It was a small place with only twenty-four patients, if that's what they were called. The nun who took charge of me was one of the modern type, in ordinary clothes and with only a small cross on a gold chain to show her allegiance.

'We try to make the surroundings as non-clinical as we can, Mr Hardy,' she said. 'Indoor plants, cheerful stuff on the walls and no obsession about tidiness.'

'And you're not overloaded with religious symbolism.'

She gave me a smile. 'Unlike what you no doubt expected. There's a chapel of course, and a cross mounted in each room, but no bleeding Jesus or saintly Madonnas.'

'It must be hard with most of them so young.'

'All,' she said. 'Yes, it is.'

We passed a couple of rooms with the doors standing open. I could see people in some of the beds, apparently sleeping. Two young men were playing cards and smoking in a sitting area. They nodded to the nun as we went past but showed not a flicker of interest in me.

'Many visitors?' I asked.

'Not enough. There's terrible ignorance about the illness. Fear of it, and a lot of shame as well. Some people are afraid to visit in case some sort of stigma attaches to them. Pierre's along here. I think you're his first visitor since the corrective services people brought him in, poor boy.'

'He was at an expensive school not so long ago. Someone must have paid. What about his family?'

'You don't know? His father was a fairly important person in the French embassy. When Pierre was expelled from the school he refused to support him. When he learned of his conviction he did nothing. When he found out about his son's illness he applied for another posting and left the country. Pierre would have been deported on the expiry of his sentence, but that's not going to happen.'

'His mother? Surely . . . ?'

The nun shook her head. 'A member of the order met her. "Hard as iron", was her judgement.'

The room bore out what she'd said. It was painted in light colours, the prints on the walls looked optimistic and the cross set up above the door was unobtrusive. The room held three beds—one was empty, someone was sleeping in another and in the third, closest to the window, a bearded man was sitting, propped up by pillows.

'Your visitor, Pierre,' the nun said.

'*En français*,' he said. 'You must practise, sister.'

'He's teaching me,' she said, 'but I'm a bad pupil. I'll leave you to it. Ring if you get tired, Pierre.'

I approached the bed and held out my hand. He took it and the bones in his hand almost crackled, although I'd put no strength in the grip. His face was skeletal, whittled down to a shell and only given any substance by the beard. He looked at the scrap of notepaper in his other hand.

'Cliff Hardy, private detective.' His accent wasn't heavy but it managed to give the words a flavour.

'That's right, Mr Fontaine.'

'Pierre, please. Take a chair. I am pleased to meet you but you should not be flattered. I would be pleased to meet *anyone*. The gaolers did not tell me why you wanted to see me. They think the dying have no more interest in life. They are quite wrong. We have more interest than ever before. You would be surprised. We read the newspapers from cover to cover and through again. We watch the television news on all the channels.'

I pulled up a chair, being careful not to let it scrape and disturb the sleeper.

'Don't be concerned,' Fontaine said. 'He's dying fast.'

He pointed to the other bed; his arm inside the pyjama jacket was stick-thin. 'Sebastian went last night. The prettiest boy he had been. He spent the last hours looking at pictures of himself taken one year ago.'

For someone who looked so frail his voice was strong and for someone nearing death he spoke with an edge of humour I couldn't help admiring. I told him about being hired to find Justin Hampshire and that I'd learned of their association at the school.

'Find Justin? *Pourquoi*? Why?'

'He went missing. He hasn't been seen for two years.'

'Ah.'

'You spent some time with him just before you ran into trouble, right?'

He nodded and the action hurt him. The look that passed over his face was like a cloud across the moon. He coughed and that hurt as well. I poured water from the jug on the bedside cabinet and handed it to him. He sipped and nodded his thanks.

'Not afraid a cough'll pass the virus?'

I shook my head.

'Some think this. *Merde*. Yes, Justin and I were friends for a little time. Not lovers, you understand. He wasn't gay.'

'Was he taking drugs?'

'Mr Hardy, I would laugh except that it would hurt me too much. No.'

'Look, Pierre, I've been told that Justin was a loner. Apart from the people he skied and surfed and snowboarded with, he didn't have any real friends. I don't see you as the sporting type.'

He smiled; he was already tiring, and this time the smile seemed to stretch the skin on his face to splitting point and force his dark eyes deeper into his skull.

'You want to know why he . . . what is the expression? Took me up?'

'Yes.'

'He was clever, you know that of course. He was paying me to teach him French. I did. He learned some quite quickly.'

'Why?'

There was a long pause and I could almost see his brain working, going back to a time when there were possibilities, a future. Then the sad shadow returned.

'He said he wanted to join the Foreign Legion.'

I thanked him, asked if there was anything he wanted that I could help with, but he was exhausted and didn't reply. We shook hands again.

Before leaving I put most of whatever I had in my wallet in the donation box.

11

So Justin wasn't gay, wasn't into drugs and had tried to learn French in order to join the Foreign Legion. That sounded like a fantasy, and the police had established with a reasonable degree of certainty that he hadn't left the country. He'd found out that neither his great-grandfather, grandfather or father were war heroes. Was that enough to turn him away from school, Duntroon and his family? Had he found out that his father was a crook?

All these interlocking questions occupied my mind along with plenty of other related ones—like, who killed Angela Pettigrew and why? And what were Paul Hampshire's chances out and about in Sydney with Wilson Stafford after him, ably and viciously assisted by Sharkey Finn? And where did I stand if my client, obviously 'a person of interest' to the police, became of more interest?

I'd walked to the hospice after driving to Darlinghurst where I had an arrangement with the owner of a house in Forbes Street. His terrace house had a side recess that I could just fit the Falcon into and he let me park there for a modest fee. After the confrontation with Stafford and his henchman, I'd taken to keeping my licensed .38 Smith &

Wesson to hand. I took it from the car and went up to the office. These old buildings have many pitfalls—poor lighting, dodgy stairs, places to hide. I observed all the precautions, feeling, when I reached the office safely, a mixture of relief and guilt at being paranoid.

For all the civility and humanity of the nun and the courage of Pierre Fontaine, the hospice experience had shaken me and I poured a solid slug of cask wine before I sat down to look at the mail and the faxes. There was nothing that couldn't wait or simply be ignored. I dug Watson's card out of my wallet and rang him. I identified myself and the indifference in his voice was packed into one word.

'Yes?'

'I wondered whether you were making any progress on the Pettigrew case?'

'What makes you think I'd talk to you about that?'

'Did you get to talk to Hampshire? I'd be interested to hear what he had to say.'

'I'm hanging up, Hardy.'

'Before you do, does the name Wilson Stafford mean anything to you?'

He didn't hang up and I enjoyed the moment and the change in his tone.

'Why should it?'

'Well, I had a meeting with him yesterday. Not a pleasant one, but one way or another things came up that might interest you.'

'Okay, Hardy, you're living up to your reputation as a pain in the arse. What do you want?'

'Just a quiet talk. I tell you some things and you do the same. Remember, I'm still looking for the missing son of a murdered woman and a man you'd no doubt describe as a person of interest.'

'I don't want you interfering.'

'I don't want to. I'm looking for mutual cooperation. Where're you based, Sergeant?'

'Chatswood.'

'That's not so far. Why don't we have a get-together over a drink later today?'

'You're pushing it.'

'I listened to the news and read the paper. You've put a tight wrap on the thing, but as I look at it you haven't got a fucking clue who killed the woman or why.'

He let go an exasperated sigh. 'Six thirty, Tosca's wine bar. See if you're a good enough detective to find it.'

He hung up. *Temper, temper*, I thought. I wrote up some notes on the meeting with Fontaine and did some more of my diagrams with the boxes and the connecting arrows and the dotted lines that meant *maybe* this related to that.

Chatswood was changing fast, with high rises springing up; the holes in the ground and cranes in the air indicated that more were on the way. I located the wine bar on the ground level of an apartment block. Not far to go for a drink, a coffee, a paper, the dry-cleaning, a bunch of flowers or a loaf of bread. Everything to hand. Thursday night. I was deliberately a bit late and the evening shoppers were having a quick one before heading home or out to eat.

Tosca's was the usual sort of place, trying to make up its mind whether it was Australian, European or American and getting everything wrong. The bottles in the wicker baskets clashed with the chrome tables that didn't harmonise with the sports prints on the walls. But there were free nuts and olives on the bar, which was a welcome sign anywhere. Watson, still in his black jacket but without the tie, sat at a corner table with an inch of red wine in his glass and a cigarette in his hand. He gave me the briefest of nods. I scoffed some nuts, bought two glasses of red and joined him.

'Thanks,' he said.

'We're off to a good start.'

'I wouldn't say that necessarily.' He stubbed out the cigarette, finished the wine in his glass and moved the other one closer. He looked tired, long hours and no result showing on his face. He glanced around, an automatic action, checking for anything he didn't like, or anyone he didn't want to see. He had all that sitting right in front of him and his attention switched back to me.

'So. What's this about Wilson Stafford?'

I drank some of the wine. Not bad, not great. A bit overpriced but I could always go back for some nuts and olives. 'Sorry, Sarge. It's a two-way street. How are you going with the investigation? Did you talk to Hampshire?'

'He's your client. Hasn't he been in touch?'

I had another pull on the drink. Didn't answer.

'Okay, you want something. We're not making progress—no witnesses, no sightings. Forensics are a zero. Hampshire showed us a copy of the record of telephone calls he made from where he was staying over the relevant time. He had two pizza deliveries and sent out for booze and an escort. He couldn't have made it to Church Point. Somehow I don't think he was in the country long enough to have had the time to organise a hit.'

'Any sign of Ronny?'

'Your turn, Hardy.'

'Right. Was there any sign that Angela Pettigrew had a lover?'

'No, not from interviews with neighbours and friends. Come on, what've you got?'

I told him that when the confrontation with Sarah and Ronny had happened, Sarah had called her mother a hypocritical bitch and Ronny had asked if I was the new bloke—implication obvious. I had a little more up my sleeve—Hampshire's hint that Sarah wasn't his daughter—but in these situations you don't show your hand until you have to. I kept that in reserve.

Watson nodded. 'That's something. Okay, no, we haven't found Ronny. What about Stafford?'

'What've you got from Sarah?'

'Bugger-all. The policewoman who's met her says she's a tough little nut under the posh school manners. Turns them on and off as it suits her. She's got a tame shrink. Won't say who he is but she reckons he says she's too traumatised to be interviewed. We have to look at her, of course. I assume she inherits and the house must be worth a bit. It's been known to happen.'

I remembered Ronny's comment that Sarah was an actress. I'd have to keep in mind that she was likely to put on a performance.

'Right,' I said, 'I need to talk to her about her brother and maybe I can get her to open up on what she meant about Angela's hypocrisy. Nearest and dearest kill each other, don't they? You have to be interested in that. You should be able to set it up for me to at least try to talk to her.'

'Jesus. All right, I'll think about it. Now what's the fucking connection with Stafford?'

I didn't give him the full rundown Templeton had given me, Hampshire was still my client after all, but I told him enough to indicate that Hampshire had played fast and loose with a dangerous man and possibly with others. Money was missing and people went looking and sometimes other people got in the way.

He lit a cigarette and considered what I'd said as he smoked and drank his wine. He didn't look very impressed but then, that wouldn't be his game. He stubbed out the cigarette.

'You're saying Hampshire's dirty?'

'I'm told he's never had so much as a parking ticket, and that's his style. My informant said he operated well under the radar.'

'Your informant being?'

I shook my head.

'Bears looking into. I'd still like to get on to this Ronny. You reckon you could get the daughter to talk about him? Or anything else useful?'

'There's a chance. She spoke to me once. But I won't kid you, I'm mainly interested in learning a bit more about her brother.'

He finished his wine. 'You realise that if what you say about Hampshire having enemies who might've killed the missus isn't just hot air, it could have implications for the disappearance of the kid.'

'I've thought of that.'

'I imagine you have, and I've thought about the missing kid as well. Two years isn't all that long. What if he turned up? What if he and his mum had words? How about that?'

'I've thought of that, too. That's why you're willing to help me talk to Sarah, and the condition will be that I ask certain questions and wear a wire. I never thought it was out of the goodness of your heart.'

Watson gave me his hard stare. 'You're a mate of Frank Parker, who just got a deputy commissioner slot, aren't you?'

'That's right.'

'It figures. He's a bleeding heart, smart bastard, just like you. I'll be in touch. Thanks again for the drink.'

'You didn't buy a round, Ian.'

He gave me the finger and left.

I went back to the bar, got another red and a handful of nuts and olives—that'd do for dinner. I felt that I was making progress of a kind but I wasn't sure in which direction. Who killed Angela? Where was Ronny? How many enemies did Paul Hampshire actually have? And what of Justin? Did all roads lead to Rome?

It wasn't early and it wasn't late. It was one of those in-between times a single person has trouble filling in. I wished I could ring Kathy, have a talk about things like surfing and sex—they went together when I was young, and maybe they would again now—but I didn't have her number. I could have rung the pub but it might have looked like pursuit, intrusion. Best to leave things the way they were.

When in doubt, work. I drove to Darlinghurst and went to the office. That meant walking through some shadowy spots at a volatile time of night when the crazies were out. I put the .38 in my pocket. A couple of trannies were walking down Forbes Street on the way to their patch on William Street at the bottom of the stairs. They gave me the invitation and I gave them a polite refusal. They seemed happy and I guess, compared to how things had been for them not so very long ago, they had reason to be. Some things had changed for the better.

The other people on my floor—the astrologer, the numismatist, the antiquarian bookseller—had gone home. In a funny way we all got along fine—marginalised semi-professionals trying to make a living in the face of scepticism, indifference and hostility. At various times we'd been close to getting together for a drink. Could have been fun, but it'd never happened.

The lights were off and as I turned on the stairwell ones they barely cut the gloom. Atmospheric. I let myself into the office. No light blinking on the answering machine but a fax had slid out and dropped to the floor. The tray had broken away some time back and that's where the sheets finished up when I wasn't around.

I picked it up and read it. Handwritten capitals: MR HARDY I'M VERY AFRAID OF THE POLICE AND EVERYTHING. PLEASE HELP ME. SARAH HAMPSHIRE.

part two

12

Watson rang me the next morning to say he'd okay'd it for me to talk to Sarah. I didn't tell him that I'd faxed her the night before to say that arrangements were being made. The fax number was the same as the one for the Church Point house. The appointment was for midday—Sarah was absenting herself from school on compassionate grounds. From what I knew of her, that wouldn't cause her too much concern.

I met Watson and a detective named Constable Kate Cafarella at the Mona Vale police station. Constable Cafarella had been spending some time with Sarah. Apparently a kindly neighbour, a Mrs Hartley, had been providing support—meals, laundry and such.

Cafarella was tall, beak-nosed, not unattractive. *Formidable*, as Pierre Fontaine might have said, but I couldn't see her as someone frightening to Sarah, who seemed pretty tough in her own way.

Watson supplied the recording device and Cafarella watched as I stripped off my shirt and taped it into place. Watson seemed a little embarrassed.

'Nothing else to do, Kate?' he asked.

'I thought I should bring Mr Hardy up to date on how things stand with Sarah.'

She wasn't hopping up and down with excitement at my manly figure, but she showed an acceptable level of appreciation.

'Thank you, Constable,' I said. I flipped on the switch of the device as I buttoned up my shirt.

'She came out of the sedation she'd been given at first, clear as bell,' Cafarella said, 'and we got nothing out of her. Nothing at all. Refused to answer the mildest of questions. Didn't kick up a fuss—no tears, no orders to piss off. Just . . . blankness. No, I'd call it a brick wall.'

Watson seemed as impressed by her account as I was, but he wanted more.

'Defensive?'

Cafarella shook her head. 'As I said—no interpretation possible.'

'Speculate,' I said.

She shrugged. 'I'd say either numb and dumb or a pretty tough cookie. Don't know her well enough to make the call.'

'That's where we're hoping Hardy can help us.' Watson checked his watch. 'Time to go.'

'Hang on,' I said. I opened my shirt enough to see the button, stopped the recording on the microcassette, rewound it and played the last few exchanges.

I gave them a bright smile. 'It's working!'

'It's been checked and rechecked, Hardy,' Watson said. 'Of course it's working. You're a clown.'

I was looking at Cafarella. 'I thought possibly my alpha rhythms or conductors might have upset the mechanism.'

'Rewind,' Watson snapped.

I did, then rebuttoned my shirt and put on my old leather jacket. I wore jeans and the shirt was faded, ex-army.

Watson and Cafarella escorted me out of the room they'd been allotted at the station. The day was cool, the reason for the jacket. They walked me to my car and Cafarella opened the door.

'How do you feel about taping a teenage girl whose mother has just been murdered, Mr Hardy? Without her knowledge?'

'Lousy,' I said.

The deal was that Cafarella would be in the house but not in earshot when I interviewed Sarah. That was okay with me; the last thing I needed was for a nymphette to play games, and I hoped it was all right with Sarah. Cafarella followed me in her car and we went up the crumbling steps with her in front. She went up easily—a runner, netball or gymnast, perhaps. Not quite Sarah's type.

'You could break your neck here,' I said. 'Or an ankle.'

Cafarella stepped neatly around two collapsed bricks. 'The path needs work all right, the garden as well. What did Sarah's mother actually *do*?'

'I never found out. Don't you lot know?'

'Ian Watson might, but on this case I'm just a female adjunct, a soother of other females. If Watson knows, he hasn't told me.'

'Did you okay this with the shrink?'

'Didn't have to. We found out the man's a charlatan, not even a doctor.'

We reached the porch and rang the bell several times

before Sarah came to the door. She addressed her greeting directly to me, ignoring Cafarella.

'Sorry, Mr Hardy. I was playing the music a bit loud.'

'The Clash,' Cafarella said. 'I heard it.'

Sarah ignored that too. 'Come in,' she said.

We went down the hallway. Sarah stopped in the kitchen. She wore jeans and a sweater, boots with a bit of heel. No makeup, but she'd washed her hair and tied it back neatly. 'Would you like some coffee or something, Mr Hardy?'

Cafarella stepped forward and, without actually touching her, made Sarah back up. 'You are a very rude girl,' she said, 'and I'm only here because I have to be.'

Sarah's stance was defiant. I said nothing.

Cafarella stepped away. 'You and Mr Hardy will sit out in the back room where I can see you from the garden. I won't be able to hear you and you can talk about whatever you bloody well like.'

She stalked away, through the sunroom and down the steps.

Sarah shrugged. 'Touchy.'

I knew it was an act on Cafarella's part, but I played along. 'They're frustrated at getting nowhere on your mother's murder. By the way, they don't know about your fax or my reply.'

Cafarella rattled the door at the top of the steps. 'You've got one hour, Mr Hardy.'

It was the signal for me to turn on the recording device. I nodded. 'Look, Sarah, I wouldn't mind some coffee—instant'll do.'

She shot Cafarella a baleful glance as she went back down the steps. 'I hate that bitch. Okay, instant. That's all I bother with anyway.'

She turned towards the shelves and I reached inside my shirt and flicked the switch.

Sarah spilled some of the powder when she spooned it into the mugs, and water sprayed out when she turned the tap on too hard to fill the jug. She got the water under control and did a fair job of making the coffee but she was clearly very troubled and I didn't think it was only about losing her mother. We went through to the sunroom and sat. The yard sloped steeply back and Cafarella must have got herself a spot towards the far end of the property where there was a rockery and garden.

'I was surprised that you wanted to see me,' I said. 'We didn't actually hit it off too well the last time.' I had to hope she wouldn't mention faxes and she didn't, quite.

'I'm frightened of the police, like I said. They think I killed Mum . . . Angela, with Ronny's help.'

'Why d'you say that?'

'I can tell. The red-headed cop asked me questions when I came out of the dope and I could see where he was going. I pretended to still be feeling it and I didn't say anything much.'

'It's the way they think, Sarah. With most people who get killed, the killer turns out to be someone close to them. You must know that from cop shows on TV.'

'I don't watch cop shows, they're dumb. I watch music and sitcoms.'

And they're not? I thought, but I said, 'As for Ronny, it's the same sort of thing. He's got a drug record.'

She took a slurp of her coffee. 'A bit of grass. Who doesn't do grass? Young people, I mean.'

'Look, I take your point. I don't see Ronny as a murderer, but it doesn't help that he's gone into hiding. If the police could speak to him and were convinced that he wasn't involved in your mother's death, that'd ease some of this pressure you feel, wouldn't it? Do you know where he is?'

'Yeah, maybe, but the police'd do him for something else, for sure—speed, carnal knowledge . . . you know. He's too scared to ring me in case the phone's bugged. I don't know why I trust you but I think I do. You're sort of different. Would you talk to him? Tell him I'm all right and that?'

Nasty moment. Just what Watson wanted to hear. Deadset betrayal, but there was no way out. I said I'd talk to him, give him her message and try to convince him to come out of hiding. For a fifteen-year-old, she had a fair bit of sangfroid. She gave what I said some thought before she nodded.

'I'll write the address down before you go—his mum's place. But that's not the main reason I'm worried.'

All this would be lapped up by Watson and Co and I was feeling worse by the minute about violating the kid's confidence. I tried to tell myself there was a murder to be solved and a boy to be found and it had to be done by hook or by crook. I had time for these thoughts because she suddenly said she needed a cigarette and got up to fetch them. She returned with one lit and the packet and lighter in her other hand. She sat, drank some coffee and took a deep drag. She seemed less of a novice than she had a few days back.

'You don't smoke, do you?' she said.

'Not anymore.'

The cigarette seemed to reassure her. Maybe it made her feel older, more able to cope.

'Want me to tell you why I'm worried about the police? Really worried?'

I nodded.

'Angela's got a boyfriend—a lover, I suppose you'd call him. She's had him for years. Even before Dad left. I'm shit-scared talking about this.'

She meant what she said and I wanted to tell her not to say any more. I wasn't the right person and this wasn't the right situation, but the words tumbled out.

'He's a politician and he was the minister for police. He's something else now, just as big. I think he probably killed Angela but I was too frightened to talk to the police about it. What if they told him and he said to shut me up or something? You can't trust the police. You must know that.'

'Some of them are all right,' I said. 'Some are actually good.'

'But they stick together.'

She was right there. I wondered whether this was some kind of fantasy, although it didn't look like it. And she had called her mother a hypocrite before any of this blew up. I wasn't sure I wanted her to put the name on tape but she did it anyway.

'It's Wayne Ireland. You wouldn't believe what they did to cover it up and I'm fucked if I know what he sees in her. He's married, with kids and his fucking career. But I know, I saw them by accident one time when I jigged school and went into the city. This was years ago and then I met Ronny.'

'What's Ronny got to do with it?'

'Ronny's dad is Wayne Ireland's driver and he's known about Ireland fucking my mother for yonks. That's sort of how we got together, Ronny and me. She's such a hypocrite, playing the suburban wifey. Shit, she worked in the public service before she got married and that must have been where she met him. He was some big union arsehole before he got into politics. Catholic, of course. She couldn't marry him so she married Dad. I suppose they had a fight then. They had a lot of fights, Ronny's dad says. He reckons she was always threatening to go public about them.'

There was a lot of hearsay in it but she was smart enough to know that the information was dangerous. She saw my hesitation and weighed in hard.

'You said she was conventional and you were right in one way but in other ways she was fucked up completely. She had frilly, girlie stuff hidden and she kept some motel bills and receipts for stuff.'

'How d'you know that?'

There was a long pause. She lit another cigarette. 'I snooped. I thought I'd blackmail her if she ever came down too heavy on me. I didn't get the chance.'

'Did your mother know who Ronny is? The connection?'

'Shit, no. I'll tell you something else. He supports her, gives her money. Did, I mean. She was a prostitute. He helped her keep her crappy business going and that's how she was able to stay in this shitty house. I wanted to go to the North Shore or the eastern suburbs, but no way. Know why?'

I shook my head.

'Because it'd put her too close to *him*! He sort of keeps . . . kept her up here, out of the way. Jesus!'

The revelation had drained her. Suddenly she seemed to be realising that her future was going to be nothing like the one she'd expected, and she started to sob. That was as much as I was prepared to take out of her for the police. I switched the recorder off as I got up to get her some tissues.

The hour was almost over. She mopped up the tears and got back to her cigarette.

'Are you going to help me, Mr Hardy? You don't go on with a lot of bullshit like most adults, and you were nice to Ronny, in the rain.'

I wanted to help her and I wanted to stay closely in touch. All this new information could have a bearing on my investigation. The idea came to me pretty easily.

'I think I can. I've got this best friend who's a policeman, very senior and completely honest. I mean completely. His wife's a great friend of mine too. Terrific people. They live in Paddington. I think you could stay with them while this gets sorted out. The police are going to have to investigate Ireland, you know that. But this is the best protection you could get.'

She nodded. 'I don't know. It sounds all right, I guess. I like Paddo, and I wouldn't have to go to that crappy school. I'll be sixteen soon, anyway.'

'There'll be a lot to sort out, Sarah. But you'll be safe with some people you'll like if I can swing it. I'm sure I can get your father's support when he's properly informed.'

She stubbed the cigarette out. 'I don't care about him. Fuck him if he doesn't agree. At least she stayed around, even though she was lying through her teeth every day. But he just buggered off.'

'Right,' I said. 'You have to remember that I'm still working for him and looking for Justin. So there's a couple of things I need to ask you before we move on. Did Justin know about your mother and Ireland?'

She dropped her head. 'Yeah. I mean, just before he went away and was acting so strange I got pissed off with him and told him everything I knew.'

'How did he take it?'

She sniffed back more tears and shook her head. 'I dunno. Bad, I guess. He was usually sort of quiet, you know. But he started yelling and carrying on. I heard Angela on the phone later making an appointment for him with Dr Van Der Harr.'

'Who's that?'

'This dopey shrink Angela made us go to after Dad left. She said we needed support after such a . . . traumatic desertion. She should've said after having two such pricks as parents. Some support—he groped me a couple of times.'

This was something new. I was sure no such name had come up in the police file on Justin's disappearance. There were questions to ask about that, when the time was right.

'Can you get me that address for Ronny?'

'Oh, sure. You won't let them heavy him too much, will you?'

I shook my head. *So much trust*—waves of guilt running through me. I reminded myself that she could be acting. If she was, she was good.

I gave her a pen and a card and she scribbled on the back of it.

'You're sure this cop and his wife are okay?'

'They're great, but I doubt they'd want you smoking grass while you're playing pool in their house.'

'They've got a pool table? That's . . .'

'Don't say it.'

She gave me a full candle-power fifteen-year-old smile. 'That's neat.'

13

Then it got tricky. I asked Sarah to pack a few things. Cafarella, having given us an extra ten minutes, came in and I told her that the information Sarah had given me could put her in danger.

'Well, we can take care of that,' she said.

'No you can't. She doesn't trust you. I don't mean you personally, but the police in general. I'm sorry but I'm going over your head. I'm calling Deputy Commissioner Frank Parker to help me make some arrangements. All I can tell you is that a very important figure is involved—not a policeman, but someone with a lot of influence in that area.'

She shook her head. 'I don't think I can allow that.'

'You have to. There'll be something in this for you and for Watson if you do as I say. If you don't it could all get very messy.'

'Jesus, you're a slippery bastard. Are you threatening us with your commissioner mate?'

'No.'

'Sounds like it. He's in Internal Affairs, isn't he?'

'That's one of his hats.'

I went into the kitchen to the wall phone and rang Frank. It took a while to get him and Cafarella fretted, unsure how to handle it. You couldn't blame her. She sneered at the cigarette butts but didn't do anything else. To keep her happy I handed her the card Sarah had written on and mouthed 'Ronny' as I hung on the line.

'Frank? Cliff. I've got a situation here that's going to need your most delicate and diplomatic touch.'

Cafarella listened as I outlined things to Frank—no names, no pack drill at this point, but I made it clear there was a high-profile suspect for the murder of Angela Pettigrew. I said that the source of the information was a minor who was fearful and that I was hoping he and Hilde would provide her with a place to stay while events unfolded.

Cafarella took this in sceptically, tapping the card against her fingernails. It wasn't as bizarre as it must have sounded to her. Frank and Hilde had a big, three storey terrace in Paddington they'd hoped to fill with children. So far, after twelve years of marriage, they had just one—Peter, my anti-godson, all of us being non-believers. Hilde had a strong maternal instinct that one child, much as she loved him, didn't satisfy. She took in strays and was happier for it. Which meant that Frank was happier.

It was all a bit like the old radio program 'Two-Way Turf Talk'. Frank agreed to contact Watson to put him in the picture, assure him that his investigation wouldn't be compromised, and to get him to contact Hampshire to reach me about the arrangement for Sarah. I spoke her name just as she emerged with a bulging overnight bag. Luckily, Cafarella had put the card away. Sarah gave her a hostile look and turned to me.

'What's happening?'

'It's coming together,' I said with the mouthpiece covered, then I said, 'Thanks, Frank,' and hung up.

Cafarella hated it. She was out of the loop, would probably have trouble with Watson. If she revealed to Sarah that I'd taped her, we could be in for a lot of conflicted shit. The phone rang and it was Watson asking for Cafarella. I handed her the phone and stepped away. I could almost hear him shouting on the line and Cafarella's knuckles whitened as she gripped the phone. She said, 'Yes, sir,' several times before hanging up.

Her lean jaw tightened. 'I'm in the shit.'

'It'll work out.'

Sarah plonked her bag down and drifted over to the window to look at the yard. 'We used to have a dog,' she said, 'but it died. I think *he* ran it over.'

Cafarella looked enquiringly at me but I shook my head. The phone rang again and it was Hampshire. He said he'd spoken to Parker and Watson and agreed to the arrangements for Sarah. He seemed dispirited, indifferent. I guess he had a lot on his mind. I got his new number.

I went to the toilet and removed the recorder. The doorbell rang and Cafarella answered it. 'Time to go,' she said.

'I'm not going with you,' Sarah said.

'Nobody asked you to. Mr Hardy's taking you to where you're going to be staying and then Mr Hardy will be part of a high-level meeting that I don't know a bloody thing about. Does that satisfy you?'

Cafarella was a tall, imposing woman, and for all her teenage pizzazz, Sarah wasn't up to coping with her anger. She didn't reply. We trooped through the house. Sarah led the way down the steps and I handed the recorder to

Cafarella. It was my second peace offering but she didn't thank me and I was pretty sure she never would.

Maintaining reasonable accord with the police is difficult in my business at the best of times, but I tried not to create outright enemies. As things stood, Watson and Cafarella were shaping up as just that.

I drove Sarah to Paddington. She was quiet, didn't smoke and seemed to be thinking about what lay in store for her. No wonder—mother dead, brother gone, father uninterested and powerful forces possibly arrayed against her. She relaxed a bit when we got over the bridge.

'Where do you live, Mr Hardy?'

'Call me Cliff. Glebe.'

'Cool. Why do you drive this old car, if you don't mind me asking?'

'I like it and when my clients see it they feel more inclined to pay my fees.'

She laughed, the first free and easy sound I'd heard from her.

I introduced her to Hilde and stayed long enough for Sarah to settle in. Everyone gets along with Hilde; she has a quality that immediately puts people at their ease and impels them to like her. Hilde made coffee and we had it out in the back courtyard, which was biggish for Paddington. Sarah dug out her cigarettes and asked Hilde if she minded.

'It's okay,' she said. 'I did it at your age, so did Frank, and I bet Cliff did, right?'

'Rollies,' I said.

'You'll quit if you're smart,' Hilde said. 'You're a very

pretty girl and it stains your teeth and isn't good for your skin, but right now isn't the time.' She slipped into a serviceable American accent. 'Bad week to give up sniffing glue.'

Sarah giggled. '*Flying High*. I love that movie,' but she lit the cigarette.

Hilde said her twelve-year-old son would soon be home and hitting the fridge. 'He's a hot pool player.'

Sarah smiled. 'We'll see how hot.'

The conference was held at the Surry Hills police centre under tight security. Present were Frank Parker; Ian Watson; his superior, Chief Superintendent Maurice Lomax; Inspector Gail Henderson, the head of the police media liaison unit; Kate Cafarella and me. Watson had cooled off about the way I'd handled things at Church Point and seen the necessity of having Cafarella there for the discussion and planning. I gathered there'd been some dispute about my participation but sanity had prevailed.

They'd played the tape through once already but ran it again when I arrived.

'Any comment, Cliff?' Frank asked.

I shrugged. 'It says what it says. Wayne has to be a person of interest.'

'He's a minister of the crown,' Lomax snapped. 'A bit of respect.'

'I'll consider respecting him when I hear he has a watertight alibi for the time Angela Pettigrew was killed.'

Gail Henderson looked up from a note she was writing. 'This has to be handled very carefully. If the press gets a whiff of an interest in Mr Ireland,' she nodded at Lomax, 'the knives will be out. Dodgy MPs sell papers.'

'Do you mind me asking what you're writing there, Gail?' Frank asked.

She held up the notebook. 'Just the names of everyone here. Am I right in thinking no one else shares this information?'

'Except Sarah and Ronny and his dad,' I said.

Watson said, 'Ronald Charles O'Connor and Michael O'Connor are both under surveillance pending the outcome of this meeting.'

Then there was a lot of procedural stuff about MPs' diaries and their drivers' log books and telephone and tax records and background checks. Angela Pettigrew had been a partner in a small firm importing ceramic ornaments from Italy. A blow from one of these—a vase I certainly hadn't noticed on my visit to the house—had killed her. The books would be looked at and a search warrant secured for the house.

'To look for the frilly stuff,' Cafarella said. 'My job, I suppose.'

'Give you a hand if you like,' I said.

The look she shot me would have made lava freeze.

Watson asked the question I'd been waiting for. 'Hardy, was there anything else she said that you didn't get on tape? I mean before or after you started recording?'

'Yes.'

Lomax, Watson and Cafarella leaned forward; Gail Henderson had her pen poised. Cafarella twigged that I was playing games and shook her head, leaned back. Watson didn't catch on. 'What?' he said.

'She said it was neat that Deputy Commissioner Parker's house has a pool table.'

Frank smiled. Gail Henderson smiled. The detectives didn't. What I'd said was almost true: I didn't think there was any need to tell them that Justin had also seen the psychiatrist Sarah had described as dopey. That had more to do with my case than theirs.

I phoned Hampshire and arranged a meeting. He wanted me to go to Crows Nest and I said I was tired of the Harbour Bridge and how about Glebe. He hesitated and I knew why. Sydney's criminal world was divided into sectors, like Berlin, and you didn't want to be in your enemy's sector. Wilson Stafford was inner west.

We agreed on Hyde Park. I walked there from where I'd left the car in Darlinghurst. I had no reason to think that Wilson Stafford had anyone watching me, but with cops and crooks always talking to each other you never know, so I took the .38 and paid very careful attention to my rear and sides on my way.

I took a seat fifty metres on from the fountain and watched the passers-by and the pigeons and the wind-blown leaves. Therapeutic. Hampshire came from the direction of St James train station. He looked very different from the jaunty figure who'd come to my office. He was tieless, wore a grey suit that didn't match his brown shoes very well. He was smoking and he stumbled over a small step in the paving. He got to my bench and sat without saying anything, breathing hard. He took a long drag on his cigarette before dropping it and stamping it out.

'Last one,' he said. 'Ever.'

'Good luck. I met up with Wilson Stafford the other day and he—'

'Jesus Christ!' He half rose and looked around as if he expected Sharkey Finn to pop out from behind a tree.

'Easy,' I said. 'You didn't tell me you had such interesting acquaintances, Paul.'

14

I told him what I'd learned from Barry Templeton about his activities before he went to America. Hampshire nodded his agreement.

'That's about right. What you don't know is that when I was flush in America I made restitution to some of those people.'

'Not to Wilson Stafford.'

'No, that was beyond me and the money I made ran out pretty quick.'

'Money made how?'

He sighed. 'The usual way. Americans can be very gullible. But it all went pear-shaped after a while.'

'That's why you came back? Because there were Wilson Stafford types in America?'

'Worse. They contract out their grievances to ruthless individuals who . . . but that's not the whole of it. The woman I took up with turned out to be a gold-digger who got very nasty when the gold ran out.'

'Which expression do you prefer—between the devil and the deep blue sea or between a rock and a hard place?'

'You're taking the piss. I suppose I deserve it. You won't believe me, but I genuinely wanted to try to get things in order—make my peace with Angela, try to find Justin. But now, with everything that's happened, I don't know.'

'You did the identification?'

'I did. The injuries were horrible. It must have been a terrible sight for Sarah.'

'Let's talk about Sarah. You implied she wasn't your child.'

'That's right. Angela wasn't faithful to me, any more than I was to her. When she fell pregnant with Sarah it was just barely possible I was the father. Unlikely though.'

'Any idea who the father might have been?'

'No. I was away a lot, in the Pacific, in the States. I had the impression there was one person in particular but I didn't know who. I didn't want to know, and I wasn't in a position to throw stones. Why are you asking?'

I expanded a bit on what I'd told him on the phone when I was getting his permission to look after Sarah. Then I'd simply said that Sarah was distressed and there were concerns for her safety. Now I said that an important person was under suspicion for Angela's death—someone capable of exerting pressure on the police.

'Who, for God's sake?'

'I can't tell you. It's under control, but the lid has to be clamped tight on it until they get more evidence.'

He felt in his jacket pocket for his cigarettes and came up with an empty packet.

'Day one,' I said. 'No, tomorrow's day one.'

'I don't think I'll make it. What happens now?'

'Up to you. I've got some leads on Justin. Nothing solid but worth pursuing—if you want to go on with it.'

'Of course I do. If you can find him it'd be something good at least to come out of this mess. But . . .'

'What?'

'What about Stafford?'

'Any chance you could recompense him to some extent? You spoke of investments. Any way to make him less unhappy?'

'Just possibly.'

'I could probably arrange a meeting for you to talk it over. At best you might be able to calm him down a bit, at worst you'd know exactly where you stand.'

'Please do it,' he said.

Without enthusiasm on either side, we shook hands and he wandered off, almost certainly to buy more cigarettes. I watched until he was out of sight. I was still on the payroll, which was good, but I was on ethically shaky ground. A meeting between Stafford and Hampshire just might cool things down and that would be good, but neither party was trustworthy. And, if I was being honest with myself, I'd have to admit that I'd welcome a chance to even the score with Stafford and Sharkey Finn. Well, there's nothing wrong with having two beneficial objectives.

I walked back through the park under the trees that showed signs of suffering from the city pollution—blotchy leaves and discoloured trunks. The water in the fountain had a tired look, but that might just have been my mood. I skirted the war memorial, a dreary, ugly structure that someone told me was only half-finished from the original design. Probably just as well.

Kathy Petersen rang me at home late that afternoon. She'd visited her grandmother and put the question to her.

'It took quite a while and a few cups of tea laced with brandy to get her talking,' Kathy said, 'but she finally told me that the scandal had to do with a Hampshire deserting in World War I. Apparently he jumped ship somewhere on the way to Gallipoli. The army contacted the family and wanted to know if he'd got back to Australia. As far as Grandma knew, he never did. The family disowned him and changed their name. There was something about it in the local paper and the family nearly died of shame.'

'It fits. Thank you, Grandma, and you, too,' I said. 'Justin found no Hampshire on the memorial. Looks like he must have gone to the Mitchell Library where he could've looked up the paper.'

'The poor kid, after all that build-up from his father. So are you getting anywhere, Cliff?'

'Hard to say. I've got someone to see who might be useful.'

'Is the Easter offer still open?'

'You bet.'

'What if you're still working on this?'

You can never tell but I had a feeling things were coming together pretty quickly. I said I'd be in the clear by Easter.

'I'll believe that when it happens. What've we got, a few weeks? I hope you find the kid and earn your fee and your time's your own. Know what? I've never seen the Blue Mountains.'

'I'll show them to you. You won't be disappointed. They're sort of blue, on a good day, when they're not grey or green.'

*

You can't get to see a psychiatrist without a referral from another doctor and then you're likely to have to wait days, if not weeks, for an appointment. I didn't have the time. A lot of people in that profession have consulting space in their houses—cuts down the overheads, especially if the wife doubles as a secretary/receptionist, and makes for a comforting atmosphere. Dr Hans Van Der Harr was in the phone book with an address in Mona Vale. It had been a long day, but I fuelled up on coffee, a couple of caffeine pills and two sausage rolls and headed north yet again.

The house was an ordinary-looking bungalow with an obviously built-on structure to one side. A pleasant garden, a car under a carport and another parked behind it. The house overlooked a golf course, which was a pleasant enough aspect, I supposed. Long way to the water though. The light was dimming when I arrived and I stayed in the car for a while, considering my strategy. A door to the added-on section opened and a man came out, hurrying, looking perhaps a little furtive. A patient most likely. He went to a newish Celica parked in the street and sat in it for a minute or more before starting up and driving off.

I got out, went to the door he'd come from and rang the bell, hoping the doctor hadn't retreated inside the house. The door opened and a tall, blonde, heavily built man stood there with a look of surprise on his face. National and professional stereotyping can lead you astray, but this man looked like a Dutchman and had a beard like Sigmund Freud's.

'I'm sorry,' he said, 'my consulting hours—'

There was no other strategy. I pushed my way in and thrust my card at him. 'I'm not here for a consultation, doctor. I'm acting for Paul Hampshire, whose wife has been murdered, whose son is missing and whose daughter is now under police protection. We need to talk.'

For a second it looked as though he would resist, but he was older than me and softer, and he decided against it. I went down a short passage past an office to a room that looked likely to be where he plied his trade—soft lighting, a recliner, two easy chairs, books, soothing prints on the walls, a vase of flowers. I sat in one of the chairs and took out my notebook. Van Der Harr hesitated, then did a good job of controlling himself. He sat in the chair furthest from me.

'I heard about Mrs Hampshire, of course, but—'

'Pettigrew. Ms Pettigrew.'

'Why are you so aggressive?'

'It's my nature. Tell me everything you can about your sessions with Justin Hampshire.'

'I'll do nothing of the sort. That's totally privileged.'

'Under the circumstances, your privilege has lapsed. How would you feel about a charge of sexually molesting an underage female?'

His calm demeanour deserted him. He blinked furiously and tugged at his beard. 'I don't know what you mean.'

'I'm sure you do, Doctor. You didn't go to the police when he went missing because you don't want to have anything to do with them, do you? Well, you don't have to if you talk to me about Justin. I warn you that I've found out a lot about him and I'll know if you lie to me.'

He made one last effort. 'This is blackmail.'

'Right, in a good cause.'

'What do you want to know?'

'Free-associate for me.'

By now he was a frightened man. He cleared his throat. 'I saw the young man three times.'

'I'll need the dates, but go on for now.'

He told me that Justin had come under protest, at his mother's insistence. That he was taciturn, resentful, uncooperative.

'He poured scorn on psychiatry, called me a charlatan. When he finally began to talk he was aggressive, threatening.'

'Physically?'

'Yes. He was big and very fit, as you are no doubt aware. He used to clench a rubber ball in his hands, presumably to strengthen them. One time when he became angry he threw it at me. It hit me on the head and it hurt.'

'What did you say to make him angry?'

'I suggested that he contact his father and try to talk to him. I believed that his problems all stemmed from that relationship. That incident happened near the end of our last session.'

'Near the end? What else was said?'

'He said that if he saw his father again he'd kill him. He had this military fantasy, as you'd know.'

'Much as I dislike doing it I'll have to ask your professional opinion. What effect would the complete demolition of that fantasy do to him?'

'Oh, that would be catastrophic. He could become violent or . . .'

'Suicidal?'

'Possibly.'

'Vengeful?'

'Very likely. In fact . . .'

'Yes?'

'He said that his father had enemies and he wished he knew who they were. At first I thought it was a delusion. I still think I was right about the relationship with the father being the source of his trouble and I would have pursued it, but . . .'

'Check your records and give me the date of that last session, then I'll go.'

I followed him into the office. He unlocked a filing cabinet, riffled through the contents and pulled out a folder. I stepped forward and snatched it from him. It had Van Der Harr's name imprinted on it and Justin's in bold letters.

'You can't take that.'

'Why not?'

'My God, you're nothing but a criminal.'

I gave him the Hardy stare and he wilted. 'You won't . . .'

'A deal's a deal,' I said. 'But I'd strongly advise you to keep your grubby hands to yourself.'

15

The encounter had been potentially useful but unpleasant, leaving a bad taste in my mouth, not through guilt but something like it. I drove home in an edgy mood. Just occasionally I had these sorts of feelings, asking myself if it was all worth it—these manipulations, this playing on people's weaknesses. The doubts didn't usually last. Hampshire wasn't much as men go, but Sarah hadn't had a fair shake and was worth helping. Above all, the boy was missing and I knew that when I focused on that, the misgivings would fall away.

I got home, poured a drink and sat down with Van Der Harr's file on Justin. I had to laugh—the psychiatrist's notes were in Dutch. As a kid I'd had a friend named Hendrik Kip, a Dutch immigrant. With some hesitation he'd told me that the word kip meant chicken. I'd picked up a few expressions and words from him as we rode bikes around Maroubra, swam and smoked furtive cigarettes, but kip means chicken was all that remained and I doubted it'd crop up in the therapist's record. All I was able to understand was the date of the last session—two days before Justin disappeared.

I put the file aside and topped up my drink. Fatigue was getting to me and I decided to put off making notes on the day until tomorrow. I finished the drink and went up to bed, trying to figure out how to get the Dutch notes translated. With Hendrik, long lost touch with, on my mind I couldn't think of a single person I knew of that nationality, let alone one who'd be happy to work on something obviously private and obviously acquired illegitimately.

When I'm on my own I can't sleep without reading for a short time, even if I'm tired and with alcohol helping. I picked up the Hughes book and read for ten minutes before feeling the heavy hardback drooping in my hands. But the question had stayed in my head and the answer came just before I fell asleep: Hilde was Swiss-German, and surely someone who can read German can read Dutch?

Wilson Stafford wasn't hard to find. He lived in Marrickville, in the nearest thing to a secure compound you can find in the inner west—a cluster of buildings inside a high wall with security gates. The site was a former timber yard and I guessed Stafford had to have pulled some strings to get the area rezoned residential. He lived there with a couple of his sons and their families, and the amount of money they spent in the locality won them influence and friends. But Stafford needed to meet people to conduct his various businesses and his favourite meeting place was a Portuguese restaurant on Addison Road.

I arrived at about twelve thirty, when Stafford would almost certainly be there, looking for his lunch. The restaurant wasn't large, flash, or fashionable, but Stafford's patronage helped to keep it running. He was there, at a table that would have seated six although only he, Sharkey Finn and another man occupied it. There were customers at two other tables. Stafford's party had bread and olive oil on the table, plus a couple of bottles of wine. Looking relaxed, until I arrived.

Sharkey saw me first, pulled himself up out of his slumped position and nudged Stafford, who looked up and went through his usual fidgety routine—cuffs, tie knot, wristwatch adjustment. He'd have been a lousy poker player. I went to the bar and ordered a glass of wine.

'Are you lunching, sir?' the barman asked.

'I'm not sure. I'm joining Mr Stafford.'

Enough said. He poured the wine and I took the glass to Stafford's table and sat down.

'What the fuck do you want?' Stafford said.

'I'm here as an intermediary. I'll explain the word for Sharkey's benefit—someone who stands between two parties to make an arrangement to suit them.'

Stafford nodded at the other man, who left the table. Sharkey fingered his wine glass—a possible weapon. Stafford leaned back and said nothing as his first course arrived—fried sardines. He tucked a napkin into his shirt front. 'Sharkey's on a diet,' he said.

'Good idea. Me too. Paul Hampshire wants a meeting. He's got a proposition for you.'

Stafford speared one of the sardines, crunched it and sighed his satisfaction. He followed it with a gulp of wine. 'Like what?'

'I don't know. Some kind of recompense. Familiar with that word, Sharkey?'

'Keep it up, Hardy. Dig your fucking grave with your mouth.'

I was trying to provoke him. He couldn't shoot me here and I was ready for him now if he came at me. As heavy as he was, well over his fighting weight, he'd be that much slower and I was set to hit him with anything to hand. But Sharkey had half a bottle of wine inside him and he knew the odds weren't good. He ignored me and got on with his drinking.

Stafford was a greedy eater; he shovelled the sardines in and wiped his plate with a chunk of bread. The smell of the food made me hungry but Stafford's table manners turned me right off. With his mouth full of bread he said, 'Do you know how much that fucker owes me?'

'No, and I don't care. I'm delivering a message.'

Sharkey snorted at that and Stafford frowned at him. He swallowed and reached for more bread which he dipped in the olive oil. 'Well, I'll talk to the arsehole. Tell him to be here this time tomorrow.'

The guy who'd been sitting at the table previously was now in a corner keeping an eye on things; the barman had reacted immediately to Stafford's name and would be on his side in any trouble. Throw in Sharkey. I shook my head. 'No chance of that, Wilson. This is your turf, you could arrange to have the place cleared of everyone except the people you've got by the balls. Somewhere neutral.'

Sharkey shook his head and this time Stafford scowled at him. *Trouble there*, I thought. *Could be useful.*

The chunk of bread in Stafford's hand dripped oil onto the tablecloth. He shrugged and the oil sprayed a bit.

'Not sure I care that much,' he said.

'You care,' I said. 'Barry Templeton told me a bit about how Hampshire took you down. Barry enjoyed telling it. You might enjoy telling him how you recouped your losses.'

'Templeton, that cunt. All right, where?'

'You suggest somewhere.'

'Marrickville RSL.'

I laughed. 'Try again.'

'Fuck you. You say.'

I drank some wine and thought. I knew Stafford wouldn't venture too far from his own stamping ground.

'I fancy somewhere with people around. Lots of them, where this punchy animal and you would have to behave. Wouldn't want to take you too far out of your comfort zone though—what about the outside area of the coffee shop at the Smith Street entrance to the Marrickville Metro? I seem to remember that the coffee's all right, and it's BYO at lunchtime. You could have a nice focaccia. Nothing for Sharkey, of course.'

'When?'

'Oh, about now tomorrow—lunchtime eaters and shoppers around. You bring Sharkey and I'll be there. Even stevens or a bit our way, allowing for Sharkey's brain damage. No weapons.'

Stafford drank some wine, did some more fidgeting and nodded. 'All right.'

I finished my wine. 'Good. Ah, here's your lunch, looks like swordfish. Good choice. Bet Sharkey nicks a chip or two. See you tomorrow and thanks for the drink.'

I phoned Hilde to say I had something she could help me with and asked after Sarah.

'She's okay. We went to the cinema last night. *Aliens*. She and Frank enjoyed it, can't say I did much—very scary. I'm glad we left Peter with a sitter. Sarah's getting on well with him and I heard her telling him all about the film—sorry, movie. She doesn't talk about her mother, but says having Peter around makes her miss her brother all over again.'

She paused as if she was going to say more and I prompted her.

'Perhaps she's a little *too* easy. I sometimes get the feeling she's acting.'

I said I was coming over and drove to Paddington, negotiated the narrow streets with their speed humps, and pulled up in front of the Parkers' house just as Sarah was coming out. She gave me a smile and lifted the shopping bag she was carrying.

'Hello, Mr Hardy. I'm going shopping, would you believe? Hilde's going to teach me to make lamb on a spoon.'

'What's that?'

'Search me. She reckons it takes eight hours to cook. Bit of a change from the TV dinners I've lived off lately. Twenty minutes max.'

'You like the Parkers?'

'Sure. Frank's a bit, you know, official. But Hilde's great, and Peter's a shit-hot pool player and a cool kid. He reminds me of Justin.'

'Pool, right—how d'you stand, head to head?'

'Dead level.' She shifted the bag to her other hand and dug in it for her cigarettes. She lit up. 'Did they find Ronny?'

'Yes, but that's all I know. If I hear more I'll tell you.'

'I'll hold you to that.' She walked off in her denim jacket, jeans and sneakers—an ordinary teenager, trailing smoke. A little further down the street a car door closed and a man stepped out and approached me.

'Constable Simpson, Mr Hardy.' He flashed his ID. 'Happy to be out of uniform for a bit. No sign of any trouble so far.'

'D'you know what to look for?'

'Everything.' He set off at a smart pace after Sarah as she rounded the corner.

I rang the bell and Hilde came to the door. A quick hug and I was in. The Parkers' house was just the way a Victorian terrace should be—uncluttered, making the most of the available space, furniture and trappings more or less in keeping with the style of the house, but in an unstudied way. I followed Hilde through to the kitchen, which was renovated but not glossy. She had been my tenant for a few years, around the time my path crossed with Frank's. I'd brought them together and the three of us were close. She knew my ways.

'A sandwich and a glass of wine,' she said. 'All ready. What's this help you need?'

I handed her the folder, sat down at the table and ate the sandwich. Curried egg—a favourite.

'Cliff, where did you get this?'

'Don't ask.'

'The man must be mad to let you even see it, never mind . . .'

'He didn't have any choice, but don't worry, he won't squawk. Great sandwich.'

Hilde shook her head as she flipped over a few pages. I drank some cold white wine, picked up a few bits of egg with my fingers and wiped my hands with a napkin. 'Can you read it? Do a rough translation?'

'Yes, of course, but I'm not sure I should.'

'Look, I don't even know if it's important. As Frank

might say, I'm trying to eliminate it from my enquiry. I'm doing everything I can to find Sarah's brother.'

She smiled. 'You bastard. You're applying pressure.'

'If it'll make you any happier, I promise I'll send it back to the shrink after I know what it says.'

She nodded. 'All right. It'll take a while. Probably a few days for me to find the time. I'll have to brush up on the differences in the languages a bit. Sort of get the feel of the Dutch. Some of this looks technical.'

'That's okay. Just give me the gist. I've got other things to do.'

'Do you think you can find him?'

It's never been my habit to ask a question like that midway through a search—it can be confidence sapping—but she forced me to it. I finished off the wine and stood.

'I don't know, love. I really don't know.' I gave her a kiss. 'Thanks for everything. I like the sound of lamb on a spoon. Invite me over for it some time, eh?'

16

I phoned Hampshire and told him the arrangements. I offered to pick him up, but he said he'd get there under his own steam. A little odd, but what wasn't in this case?

'I'll arrive a bit early then,' I said, 'to check things out. It'd be best for you to be just a shade late.'

He agreed and rang off. He sounded reasonably steady given his many problems. He didn't mention Sarah.

I called Frank in the evening and asked him how the investigation into Wayne Ireland was going. I knew it wouldn't be easy. My knowledge of Ireland was sketchy, amounting to nothing more than being aware that he was part of the right-wing machine, with all that implied about connections to unions and the tougher elements in politics and business. He was the minister for transport—middle ranked but influential.

'Can't tell you, Cliff, you know that.'

'A hint.'

'It's ongoing, as they say. Sarah asked me about Ronny and I told her that he wasn't being held. I also advised her to have no more to do with him.'

'How did she take that?'

'Pretty well. She's not a bad kid. Gets on very well with Hilde and Peter. It's sort of nice to have her around. She pitches in.'

'I met Simpson outside today when I came over. Simpson without his donkey.'

'Jesus, Cliff, you'd joke on your deathbed.'

'Never happen. Anyway, I saw Sarah and she seemed fine. I'm grateful for your help, Frank.'

'You should be. As usual, you're on a long leash with me, but I hope you haven't been talking out of turn—to your client, for instance.'

'Not a word. If the Ireland case gets to court Sarah's in for a rough time, wouldn't you say? Be a help if I can locate her brother.'

'Stay with it, and for Christ's sake try to make it somewhere near the legal line.'

He hung up. Did his last remark mean that Hilde had told him about the Van Der Harr file on Justin, or was it simply a comment on my usual methods? Hard to say. He seemed to think I'd paid my visit just to see Sarah. I didn't like keeping things from him, but then, he was certainly keeping things from me.

I got to the appointed meeting place ten minutes early and hung around looking for signs of dirty tricks—people the old-time detectives would have called wrong 'uns, male or female, or weapons stashed in rubbish bins or in the shrubbery. It all looked clean. Stafford and Sharkey arrived on time and sat at one of the tables nearest the coffee shop door. There was a sports store opposite and a short covered walkway into the mall. One of the other three outdoor tables was occupied by a woman with a child in a pram. People were going in and out of the shopping centre. Not a lot, but enough. The area was paved and clean—a few drifting leaves, the odd bit of paper.

'There's no table service, boys,' I said as I marched up to the pair. 'Allow me. What'll you have? Water for you, Sharkey?'

'Don't fuck around, Hardy. Where is he?'

I checked my watch. 'He's being fashionably late. We can't sit here without buying something.'

'Long blacks,' Stafford growled, 'and he's got five minutes, tops.'

I went into the coffee shop, ordered four long blacks and watched out through the window as they were prepared. I carried them out on a tray just as Hampshire arrived. He was dressed smartly—grey three-piece suit, tie, high-shine shoes—and he was leading on a leash the nastiest-looking dog I'd ever seen—a pink-eyed, pig-snouted pit bull.

'What the fuck is this?' Stafford roared.

'Just a little insurance, Wilson,' Hampshire said. He sat and tied the leash to his chair.

I was so surprised to see the dog, so appalled by its ugliness, that I took my eye off Sharkey. He'd retained some of his ring quickness—I'd been wrong about that. In no more than a couple of seconds he was back with a baseball bat he must have grabbed in the sports store. He took one swing, timed it perfectly as the dog leapt at him and crushed its skull. Blood, brain matter and bone sprayed in all directions as the dog gave a strangled groan and collapsed. Women and children screamed, men yelled. Sharkey had almost overbalanced with the violence of his swing, but he recovered quickly and Hampshire was clearly his next target.

I launched myself, carrying the table and its contents with me, and cannoned into Sharkey when he was halfway through his swing. He staggered, lost balance again, and I was up before him. I hit him with a right hook as low as I could reach. Not quite low enough: it hurt but didn't disable him. He sucked in air, ignored my next punch and grabbed me by the jacket, pulling me close. He was roaring, spitting, and the saliva hit my face, but he was still a boxer and his instinct was to punch. I brought my knee up hard and caught him solidly in the balls. He yelled and lost his grip as the strength drained out of him. He was still dangerous though, reaching for the baseball bat. I picked it up and slammed it into his right kneecap.

I was breathing hard. That kind of violence affects people in different ways—some become half demented, others stay icy calm. I was somewhere in between. When I looked around I saw that the area had almost cleared, with a couple of people pressed back against the walls and some coffee shop patrons with their noses stuck to the glass. There was no sign of Stafford or Hampshire. I grabbed a napkin from the ground, wiped down where I'd gripped the bat and dropped it. The place was a mess with the dead dog and a writhing Sharkey, broken crockery, upset furniture and spilt coffee mixing with the blood. I walked away.

A man and a woman came down the path from the street and stopped when they saw me.

'Call an ambulance,' I said. 'Bit late for the vet.'

*

I drove to the office and, as I'd half expected, Hampshire was waiting for me in the street.

'Got anything to drink up there, Hardy?' he said. 'I need something after that.'

'Wine,' I said.

'That'll do.'

We went up and I poured us each a decent slug of the rough red. Hampshire socked it straight down and held out the paper cup.

'Take it easy,' I said as I topped him up.

He drank only two-thirds this time. 'Did you ever see anything like that in your life?'

'Not exactly, but I've seen worse—substitute a woman for the dog.'

'My God.'

'You're playing with rough people, Paul. What was the idea?'

'I felt I needed protection.'

'Thanks for the vote of confidence.'

'I'm sorry. I didn't realise you were so . . . capable.'

'Where did you get the dog?'

'The same place I got the car, from a friend. One of the few I've got left. I guess I won't have him anymore.'

I drank some wine and felt it soothe me. 'You didn't really intend to negotiate a deal with Stafford, did you?'

'No. I just wanted to size him up, see how serious he was. I didn't get the chance.'

'He'll come after you, mate. He'll turn the town upside down.'

'I know. I'll have to leave. I'm not safe here.'

'You're not safe anywhere. Does anyone else know where you're staying? I don't even know.'

'Just the police.'

I groaned. 'Stafford's got a few of them in his pocket. There's a place in Glebe I've put people in, a motel. They know the score. It's the best I can come up with for the moment. Where's your car?'

'Down in St Peters Lane—illegally parked.'

'No time to lose. I'll get you to the motel and then we'll think it through.'

'I have to piss.'

I showed him where and told him to be quick about it. He wasn't. When he came back he gulped down the rest of his drink. 'Sorry, I guess I know why they say shit-scared.'

I took the ancient sawn-off out of the cupboard and we went down the stairs, me leading. I could almost feel the way his feet faltered on the steps. A very frightened man and I wasn't sympathetic.

St Peters Lane is a narrow one-way street with a sharp bend halfway along, and it's bordered on one side by a high stone wall surrounding a church property. There's no parking, no footpath, and it doesn't take you anywhere you can't get to more comfortably by another route. That day there were a few cars jammed up against the wall. Not unusual. Joy-riders stole cars in the suburbs to get into the Cross and then dumped them; bombs out of registration, stripped of their plates, found a temporary home there.

Hampshire was struggling to regain his composure and confidence.

'Where are you?' he said.

'Forbes Street.'

'I'll follow you.' He jiggled his keys, pointed to an iridescent blue Holden ute fifty metres away, and headed towards it.

Just then a big 4WD came screaming around the bend, going the wrong way, accelerating. Hampshire didn't have a chance. The bulky vehicle hit him full square, lifted him up and threw him against the high church wall like a bull tossing a toreador.

The shottie was useless and, when I reviewed the scene in my mind later, I got no solid impressions of the vehicle or the driver. A dun-coloured Land Cruiser, maybe. Baseball cap, sunglasses, maybe. I went across to where Hampshire lay in a spreading pool of blood. There was no pulse. His body was broken almost everywhere it could have been broken and his head was pulped, with the face nearly obliterated. The church wall was smeared with blood and the pink-grey of brain tissue.

I went back to my office, stowed the shotgun and called the police.

part three

17

I had to tell the police practically everything about my dealings with Hampshire and Wilson Stafford. I described the meeting as an attempt at reconciliation between the two that had gone badly wrong on both sides.

A few witnesses identified me as the person who hit Billy Finn, but each of them said it was in self-defence after Finn's attack on the dog and threat against Hampshire. The talk of charging me with assault fell away. Finn didn't want to press charges, and he was busy battling public nuisance, affray and similar accusations himself, as well as undergoing surgery and rehabilitation for his knee.

I heard later that a police board suggested my licence be suspended, but when it was revealed that Sharkey had been carrying a loaded, unregistered pistol, the suggestion wasn't acted on. The police had no time for Sharkey.

At the pub I ran into one of the Glebe detectives who'd got the story on the grapevine. I prepared myself for a serve but he insisted on buying me a drink. He was drunk.

'Fuckin' good work, Cliffo,' he said, 'wish you'd busted his other fuckin' knee while you were at it.'

'The trouble is, he'll mend,' I said.

'Yeah. Tell you what, though—I wouldn't like to be you at the fuckin' inquest.'

After what I told the police about their dealings, Wilson Stafford was under suspicion of organising Hampshire's killing, but he denied it and there was no evidence to go on. My identification of the vehicle and driver amounted to almost nothing, and no sign of either had so far been found.

Meanwhile, through all this, when I was in and out of police stations and on the phone every other day to Viv Garner, Wayne Ireland was charged with the manslaughter of Angela Pettigrew. Michael O'Connor, Ireland's driver, admitted driving him to the Church Point house at the time in question and to falsifying his log in return for a consideration. Ireland accused O'Connor of lying and of blackmailing him. Ireland presented medical evidence of his alcoholism and depression and was released on bail with his passport confiscated.

'Never get him for murder,' Frank Parker told me. 'Too many big guns on his side and too much medical flak. At best he'll do three or four years somewhere soft—get off the grog and work on his golf. Do himself a world of good.'

'It's the end of his political career and his marriage, though,' I said. 'And Sarah'll have to give evidence. Do you think she's still in danger?'

'I doubt it. Ireland knows he'll slip through the cracks. How about you, Cliff? You haven't got a client anymore.'

That was true and uncomfortable. I couldn't afford to work pro bono for very long, and Paul Hampshire's death had received considerable newspaper and television coverage. If Justin was still around there was a better than even chance he'd have got wind of it and made contact. It wasn't looking good for the kid who'd had his past and future taken away from him. But it left the question of what had happened to him—a serious loose end with emotional attachments.

I visited Sarah in Paddington and found her calm.

'I'm sorry he died like that, but he wasn't ever like a father,' she said. 'He wasn't around much and he didn't seem to care about me. I don't think I'm his daughter.'

Hampshire had thought the same but it wasn't the moment to tell her that.

'You know who I think my father is, don't you?'

'I can guess.'

She showed me a newspaper photo of Ireland as a young man.

'Him,' she said. 'The guy who killed my mother. Well, he didn't want to know me either, so I don't care about him.'

'This is all very hard for you,' I said.

She shrugged. 'Not really. It sort of clears the air. I'm on my own now and I can make a fresh start without all the lying and bullshit they went on with. I'll be all right.'

'Any idea what you'll do?'

'I don't know. Maybe I'll be a private detective.'

'I wouldn't advise it—too much to do for too little money.'

'Do you think you'll find Justin? I hope you can. At least I know he's my half-brother. If we could get together maybe we could work something out.'

'I'll keep looking,' I said.

*

Pierre Fontaine died in the hospice. I went to the service and the cremation on the off-chance that Justin might show. He didn't. I was running out of options. I thought of Ronny O'Connor. Was there anything more to be squeezed out of him? I doubted it. It looked like a dead end and I hated it. I felt I'd failed Paul Hampshire, even though he'd never been straight with me.

Then Hilde phoned me and the whole thing took on a new shape. 'Oh, Cliff,' she said, her voice breaking, 'I've been such a fool. I left that psychiatrist's file on my desk, just for a few minutes, and Sarah must have seen it. She took it. She's gone, Cliff. She's gone!'

I calmed her down, told her it was my fault for making it possible for Sarah to see the file and asked her to describe what Sarah had been wearing and what she'd taken with her. She said Sarah had been in her jeans and denim jacket, exactly as I'd last seen her, and that she'd taken the overnight bag she arrived with.

'Has she got any money?'

'She's got a keycard. She seemed to have enough to get by day to day. She never asked us for money. Cliff, what am I going to say to Frank? I didn't tell him about the file.'

'I'll ring him and explain. I'll take the blame.'

I rang Frank and told him what had happened. 'Jesus, Cliff, you bloody fool.'

'I know. Sorry.'

'And Hilde's a fool for helping you. Why she has you up on a pedestal I'll never know.'

'Me either. The important thing now is to find Sarah.'

'You're the expert. You'd better do it. If she comes to any harm this could turn very nasty for all of us. Gail

Henderson in media liaison says there's already a journalist sniffing around.'

'Who?'

'Her name's Tania Kramer, a freelance nuisance.'

I rang Hilde, told her I'd spoken to Frank and asked her if Sarah had taken any phone calls recently.

'She did, this morning. A woman asked for her. She said she was a friend.'

'What name?'

'Tania. Sarah spoke to her for a few minutes, or rather she listened. What's going on?'

'I'm not sure, but that's a lead to follow.'

'What did Frank say?'

'He called us both fools, but more me than you.'

She was close to tears. 'Peter wants to know where she is. Jesus, Cliff, this is affecting a lot of people.'

'It's always like that,' I said.

I knew Tania Kramer. A couple of years back she'd written a series of articles about a case I'd been involved in. She pestered me for information and, when I wouldn't come through, she made all sorts of wild assumptions about my role in the matter. Viv Garner advised me to sue her and the paper she'd published in and walk away with big damages.

'You've heard of the Murdoch boat and the Fairfax beach house,' Viv had said. 'She's libelled you. You could clean up.'

'And get the whole thing a new run in the papers,' I said. 'Let it go. It'll all be forgotten by next month, next week.'

Tania was an attractive woman and she'd tried to use that. She'd invited me to her place for a drink and I'd gone, had the drink and that was all. She lived in Newtown in a big house overlooking Hollis Park. She'd come away with the house from a marriage to a stockbroker. She had a mortgage, she'd told me, and took in tenants, but she was doing well as a freelancer and sitting comfortably in a very desirable place to live. I found her card in the box I keep for such things, rang the number and got her answering machine. I didn't leave a message.

Hollis Park was like a London square, with big houses flanking the grass and gardens on two sides. The houses were smaller and more modest on the other sides. The terraces hadn't been changed too much aside from the odd built-in balcony. The park itself was a bit scruffy and could have done with a thorough renovation.

After my visit to Tania Kramer, I'd looked Hollis Park up in a directory because I was impressed by the place. Apparently it was designed and built by a magistrate in the 1880s. I wondered how he'd made the money. It was a fair bet that he'd occupied the best of the biggest houses himself.

Tania's place wasn't the biggest but it had been well maintained and didn't let the elegant layout down. I parked in a side street and walked through the park. I opened the gate and climbed the impressive sandstone steps to the tiled front porch. The garden was lush and showed signs of being well-planned and cared for. I rang the bell and heard it sound inside the house. I'm a knocker man myself; easier to ignore than a bell.

Tania opened the door. It had been a few years but she was ageing well. A touch of grey in the sleek, dark hair, a few lines, but she still had a lean, upright figure and knew how to dress—white blouse, dark pants, heels.

'Cliff,' she said, 'how nice to see you. Come in.'

I followed her down the broad passage with its carpet runner and wood-panelled walls.

'Not a bit surprised, are you, Tania?'

'Not at all. I was expecting you, although you're here a little sooner than I thought. That was you ringing and not leaving a message, right?'

'Right. Is Sarah here?'

'She certainly is, and doesn't she have a story to tell. You've gone out on a limb here, my friend, you and a few others.'

There was no arguing with that. We reached the end of the passage and went up the stairs.

'A few changes since you were here last,' she said. 'I have the top floor all to myself.'

'I'm the same,' I said. 'With the bottom floor as well.'

'In a grotty little dump in Glebe.'

'Water view.'

'Glimpse—through apartment blocks. How's your wind?'

We reached the third level and there was ample evidence of renovation and money spent. Polished floors, skylights, a living area that had been opened out by the removal of a wall or two.

'You've won a lottery,' I said.

'Paid off the mortgage, darling. It's downhill all the way. Take a seat. I'll get Sarah.'

The room featured well-stocked bookshelves, a cane lounge suite with padded cushions, big screen TV with VCR and an elaborate hi-fi set-up. No bar, that'd be vulgar; no drinks tray, that'd be pretentious. Tania had taste to equal her ambition and ruthlessness.

'Hello, Mr Hardy.'

Sarah appeared as if from nowhere. The angry schoolgirl and the tough teenager had vanished. She still wore her denims but at a guess she'd been at Tania's makeup kit. She looked older, more composed. At least superficially, she'd achieved a new level of sophistication. It didn't surprise me that a few hours in the company of Tania could produce that. Sarah sat opposite me on the couch and lit a cigarette.

'I trusted you,' she said. 'I don't anymore.'

'I'm sorry. Why not?'

Tania came in with a coffee pot, cups, cream and sugar on a tray. 'You know why, Cliff.'

'Van Der Harr's file on Justin. I can explain that.'

'I'm sure you can.' Tania gave Sarah an encouraging smile as she poured the coffee. 'But it's more than that. I got a leak of your statement to the police. You knew Paul Hampshire doubted that Sarah was his daughter, but you didn't say anything about it to her when you spirited her away to live with your mate and your ex-girlfriend.'

That was typical of Tania. She loved the obvious, doubted the nuances, made assumptions and treated them as facts. It wasn't worth your breath to correct her, she didn't hear anyway. Anyway, she was right that I'd withheld information from Sarah but I didn't feel bad about that.

'I didn't want to add to Sarah's anxieties,' I said. 'She was very vulnerable.'

'Does she look vulnerable to you now?'

'What's going on, Tania? What's your interest in this?'

Tania took a cigarette from Sarah's packet and lit it. They exchanged conspiratorial smiles. 'The story, of course,' she said. 'Sarah's story. There's a book in this. A best-seller. A lot of money to be made.'

'You're a cold-blooded bitch, Tania. Sarah won't need it. She'll inherit her mother's house. It's worth a lot of money.'

Tania tapped off her ash. 'Temper, temper. That's where you're wrong. Tell him, Sarah.'

'Angela and I fought a lot. You knew that.'

I nodded.

'One day we had a real beauty, over school and all the shit she made me put up with. We really slammed into each other. She showed me a copy of her will. She's left everything to be equally divided between me and Justin.'

'Who's been missing for two years and a bit,' Tania said. 'But it takes a fair while longer than that to have the authorities declare someone dead, unless there's some very solid evidence. Means everything would be tied up for quite a while.'

We hadn't touched the coffee. I drank some now to ease a dry throat. 'True,' I said.

Tania smiled. 'That's where you come in, Clifford.'

18

It was bizarre. Tania and Sarah wanted me to continue to look for Justin, either to find him or provide good reason to have him declared dead.

'The story needs an ending,' Tania said.

'You mean you need it to do this best-seller.'

'Same thing. Damn, this coffee's cold.'

'Suppose I just chuck it, cut my losses?'

Sarah stubbed out her cigarette. 'You won't.'

'Why did you take off like that, Sarah? I know Tania must've sweet-talked you over the phone, but . . .'

'I went right off when I saw that fucking file on Hilde's desk. Like I told you, that dirty bastard copped a feel a couple of times. I couldn't believe that you'd have anything to do with him.'

'Listen, I left him whimpering. Didn't mention you by name, but I pressured him by threatening a charge of molesting an underage female. He was shit-scared. I stole the file because I hoped it might tell me something useful about Justin, but it's in Dutch. Hilde reads German and she can manage Dutch. I was getting her to translate it for me.'

Sarah nodded. 'Yeah, I see that now. But with everything going on, and feeling so good about being with the Parkers and then seeing that fucker's name, I just flipped.'

Tania was wearing a triumphant smile. 'I can take some of the credit,' she said. 'I told Sarah to bring anything she could that might have a bearing on the story. She was going to rip the file to shreds. I told her not to.'

'Credit?' I said.

'Credit. Where d'you think I got the name Kramer from? My father was a German immigrant. I grew up bilingual. I can read Dutch as well as your ex-girlfriend.'

'Knock it off, Tania. She was never that.'

Tania shrugged. 'Who cares? The point is, you were right. There is something in that paedophile's notes that could be useful.'

'Where's the file now?'

'Safe,' Tania said. 'You nicked it once, can't let you do it again. You could be in trouble over that—theft, menaces . . .'

'Van Der Harr wouldn't risk the exposure.'

Tania shrugged. 'You never know, and it wouldn't look good if I chose to write it up that way.'

I almost had to admire her. She'd missed her calling—should have been in ASIO or some other dirty tricks outfit.

'Nothing to say, Cliff?'

'You're doing all the talking.'

'Justin told the psychiatrist that he knew his father had enemies.'

'I know that. Van Der Harr said so.'

'Did he give you a name?'

That hit home. Tania and Sarah looked pleased with themselves and I thought back to my meeting with Van Der

Harr. Something stirred in my memory. What had he said? *At first I thought it was a delusion . . .* I'd been so keen to get the file and get away from him that I hadn't followed through on what his statement implied.

'No names,' I said. 'I doubt Justin could've found out anything like that.'

Sarah gave me a dirty look. 'Justin was very smart.'

'Right,' Tania said.

I was getting tired of the fencing. 'There are a lot of people smarter than me in this world, Tania, but you're not one of them. Why don't you just come out with it and let me decide whether it's worth anything or not.'

Tania shook her head. 'No, we want to make sure you're going to follow this up and give it all you've got. A lot depends on it—not just the book and Sarah's inheritance, but other things as well.'

'Like what?'

'I hear there was talk of suspending your licence. You're on thin ice, I'm told. Stealing a doctor's files, threatening him, doing dodgy deals with the cops . . .'

It was time to try a bit of divide and rule. 'You've already played that card, Tania. If Justin's smart, so is Sarah. She knows that it was a good move for her to go to the Parkers. You won't manipulate her into making life hard for them.'

Tania betrayed doubt for the first time by reaching for another cigarette. 'I . . . we . . . just want to make sure . . .'

'I want to find Justin as much as you do. I've done a lot of work on what threw him off beam and, believe me, what he found out was enough to shake anyone up. Particularly a youngster who'd been fed so many lies.'

'What?' Sarah said. 'What?'

Tania could see what was happening and she tried to

recover ground. 'You should have looked through Van Der Harr's notes more closely, Cliff. Sure they were in Dutch, but didn't you notice the name Wayne Ireland?'

I hadn't noticed. Monolingual, I'd been completely put off by seeing pages of handwriting in a foreign language.

Tania recovered ground well. 'Some detective,' she said.

I turned to Sarah. 'You said you told Justin about Ireland.'

She nodded.

'So he knew about him and your mother but why would he think that Ireland and Paul Hampshire could be called enemies? Hampshire knew nothing about Ireland.'

'Now you're talking like a detective,' Tania said. 'That's what you've got to look into. Did Justin go to see Ireland and if he did, what happened next? See? This is the stuff the story needs and we need to know to find out what happened to Justin.'

'You're assuming a lot,' I said.

Tania took a deep draw and blew out the smoke in a theatrical stream. 'Fucking right I am.'

I hated to admit it, but she'd opened up a legitimate avenue of enquiry. It wasn't like Tania to delegate, though. I asked her why she didn't try to get to Ireland herself. She stubbed out her cigarette and looked uncomfortable, but just for a second.

'That man is a complete arsehole,' she said. 'I interviewed him once about something to do with his portfolio. Talk about a sleaze. He was all over me. Those ALP shits are all like that—half pissed on beer most of the time, with their haitches and their somethinks and everythinks.'

'Doesn't sound like your cup of tea, or Angela Pettigrew's, for that matter,' I said.

'Oh, he'd smoothed off a lot of the rough edges. Bit of a chameleon, really. One thing with the merchant bankers and another with the union brothers. He knew some heavy types, all right, and he told me about them. But he was always a pants man. A bit too pleased with himself for me. I was lucky to get away with my bra on.'

Sarah thought that was funny and laughed. Tania didn't and scowled at her. Divide and rule. Tania's politics and class prejudices were showing. Always useful to know. Time to go, nearly, with one important thing to clear up.

'What's Sarah going to do?'

Tania smiled sweetly. 'I've already spoken to Sarah's aunt on her mother's side. Sort of half-sister, half-aunt. She doesn't want to be involved but she says she'll endorse my submission to social services for Sarah to stay here.'

'What about school?'

'There're plenty of schools around here.'

'I want to stay with Tania,' Sarah said.

I got up. 'I'll make your excuses to Hilde.'

'I'm sorry,' Sarah said. 'I . . .'

'Yeah,' I said. 'I'll see myself out, Tania, and be in touch. Tell you what—better get in a pool table.'

It was a cheap shot but they'd irritated me. Tania's agenda was plain to see and she didn't give a shit about finding Justin except as a chapter in her book. Sarah was a different proposition and difficult to read. Growing up with an indifferent father and a mother leading a double life had to have an effect on a young person's outlook and behaviour. She appeared to be coping well with the pressures, but that only raised the question of when she might crack.

I stood outside the house looking over the park as two kids threw a frisbee around with considerable skill. I hadn't seen a frisbee in a while. Another fading fad.

19

When I got back to the office I found that Tania had faxed through a brief translation of the relevant passage in Van Der Harr's notes: *Subject says intends to contact father's enemy named Ireland to cause father harm. Agitated, disturbed, delusional?* That was pretty much in line with what the psychiatrist had told me. It could prove useful or be a dead end, but one question persisted: how did Justin come up with the idea that Ireland was Hampshire's enemy?

I sat down with my notebook and went through my usual routine of referring to the notes of interviews and scribbled comments, writing down names, boxing them in, joining them with arrows or dotted lines according to the strength or weakness of the connections. It usually ended up like a dog's breakfast and wasn't helpful, but this time it was. The connection between Justin and Ireland ran through Ronny O'Connor and his father, Michael. Not strong, but there.

Tackling Wayne Ireland was going to be difficult and it was important to test Van Der Harr's suggestion that Justin was delusional. Was he just mixing up his mother's adultery with his father's many failings? Or had he come across something solid? Michael O'Connor was scheduled to be a witness against Ireland when he came to trial. That could be a long time off. If Ireland was acquitted, O'Connor was a sitting duck, up for a perjury charge. He must have lost his job. Couldn't be happy, maybe willing to talk, but there was no chance the police would tell me where he was.

Contacts are everything in this line of work and, while I didn't know anyone in charge of the government car pool, I did know the boss at the place in Paddington where they were serviced. He was a fan of old Falcons and I'd been referred to him when it looked as though the state of mine might be terminal. It wasn't: Todd Hawker brought it back to life at a cost almost equal to its value overall.

I bought a six-pack of Reschs Pilsener and drove to Paddington, parking in one of the bays reserved for cars being worked on.

'Hey!' a mechanic working close by shouted.

'I'm here to see Todd,' I said. 'Won't be long.'

He ducked his head back under the bonnet and fiddled with something. The workshop was busy, with three cars up on hoists and machinery running. To get to Todd's office you have to step over tyres, gear boxes and other car parts and try to keep yourself clear of grease and oil slicks. Todd wasn't a desk wallah; he wore overalls and got them and himself dirty. He was sitting at his desk totally absorbed in a batch of invoices. I entered quietly and put the beer down in front of him.

He looked up. 'Oh, Christ, Cliff Hardy with baksheesh. What is it, a master cylinder again?'

'Nothing mechanical, mate,' I said. 'A tiny scrap of information.'

He broke the plastic wrapping, pulled out two beers and pushed one towards me. We took the tops off and touched bottles.

'Information?'

'You know Michael O'Connor—drives for Wayne Ireland, or did.'

Todd drank a third of the beer in a gulp. 'I know him. A real prick. What's he done?'

'This and that. I need to talk to him. Got an address?'

Another gulp lowered the level. 'Why would I have an address? I don't send him any fuckin' invoices. The government pays for the work on the cars—you and me, that is. I've got a home phone number, but.'

I was enjoying the beer, taking it more slowly. 'That'll do.'

Todd finished his drink, got a notebook from the drawer and thumbed through it. He found the number and I wrote it down.

'You say he's a prick. Anything specific?'

'He asked me to inflate the price of the work on his boss's car. Said he could get it passed and we'd split the difference. I told him to fuck off. A few of them come it, but he was a bit persistent. Tried it on with the petrol, too. Greedy bastard. I only do the government's cars. Another mob does the Opposition's. I bet it happens with those cunts. Me, I'm public spirited.'

'And like you say, we pay for it. Labor's in trouble, though. What'll you do if the Liberals take over?'

'No worries. They'll take the work off me for sure. I'll switch over with a bit of luck.'

I thanked him, we talked politics briefly and I left. It's not easy these days to find a telephone booth with an intact phone book but I got lucky a few blocks from Todd's garage. Intact enough, anyway, for me to check on the M O'Connors. There was a column and a half of them, but the phone number did the trick. Michael, the admitted conniver or the alleged blackmailer, father of Ronald, lived in The Rocks. Very nice, and handy to Parliament House.

I drove to The Rocks, found a parking place and fed the meter. I drew five hundred dollars from an ATM, just about the last of Hampshire's retainer.

O'Connor's sandstone cottage was in the shadow of the bridge in what looked like a heritage-protected, rent-controlled area of the precinct. Maybe a perk of his job. Right time to catch him because if that was true he'd be leaving soon. I hadn't rehearsed my approach—sometimes spontaneity was the way to go. The cottage sat straight on the street. I used the knocker and when the door opened I was looking at Ronny.

I had a foot and a shoulder inside as he stepped back. 'Gidday, Ronny old son,' I said. 'Your dad in?'

'The fuck do you want?'

I kept moving so that I was completely inside. 'What kind of a way is that to talk to the bloke who gave you a lift and a packet of fags?'

I pushed on down the passage and he retreated. 'And belted me and dobbed me in to the cops.'

'It was just a tap, and when Sarah's mother was killed I didn't have any choice about talking to the cops. For what it's worth, I told them I was sure you hadn't done it.'

Ronny wasn't at his best: he was unshaven, probably under-slept and he smelled of beer and dope, but he wasn't without some spirit. 'Why not? I hated the bitch.'

'You're not the type, and don't try to be the type, you won't make it. I want to talk to your father.'

'He's crook.'

'I imagine so. He's facing goal. Does he need money?'

Ronny wasn't so out of it not to respond to that. 'Yeah, I suppose.'

I'd kept him moving and we were in a living area now, with a door off it and a kitchen further down. Michael wasn't the neatest keeper of a heritage home. The place was a junkyard of decaying furniture—a couch with a tangled blanket, empty bottles, collapsed wine casks and dirty clothes.

'Just out of interest, how come you went to Bryce Grammar and were up around there?'

He shrugged. 'My mum paid and I lived with her on and off. Another stuck-up bitch. Got any smokes? I'm out.'

'Where's your father?'

He pointed to the door. I handed him a five-dollar note. 'I won't hurt him. Give me half an hour.'

'Do what the fuck you like.' He took the money and he was gone.

I pushed the door open and went into a bedroom that looked bad and smelled worse. A man was lying on the single bed; he was snoring and he twitched when a shaft of light from the open door hit him. Twitched, but didn't wake up. The room shrieked neglect—clothes on a chair and the floor, beer cans on the dresser, wardrobe doors open with shoes, newspapers and bed linen spilling out. A chamber pot, half full, stuck out from under the bed. An ashtray on the bedside table overflowed with butts.

Michael O'Connor was a flabbier version of Ronny. The same sharp features were being swamped by beer fat.

His second chin wobbled with every snore. His singlet was ash-stained; a four-tooth dental plate sat next to the ashtray. Drivers for politicians had to present smartly; this one had come down very far, very quickly. I pushed clothes from the chair and pulled it up near the bed before pinching O'Connor's nose shut between my thumb and forefinger. He gave a snort and a wave of foul-smelling breath came from his mouth as he gulped for air.

'Wake up, Mick,' I said. 'You've got a visitor.'

His bleary eyes opened and focused briefly before closing again. I reached over to the dresser and found a can that still held some beer. I poured it over his face. He spluttered and woke up fully.

'What the fuck d'you think you're doing? Who are you?'

I showed him my card. He blinked several times before he was able to read it.

'Fuck off.'

'Close your eyes again and I'll empty the pot of piss over you.'

He struggled to sit up, wrestling a grubby pillow into place. 'What do you want?'

I took out the money, fanning the notes. 'I'm paying for information.'

That got his attention. He fumbled for his denture and shoved it in, grey flecks and all. He looked for cigarettes.

'Ronny's gone for some,' I said. 'I gave him five bucks. Maybe he'll share.'

'He better. The little prick's smoked all mine. What's this about?'

'Angela Pettigrew and Paul and Justin Hampshire.'

'Jesus, I told the police all I know about that.'

'And your boss says you're a liar. I couldn't care less one

way or the other. I want to know how Justin Hampshire knew that Wayne Ireland was his father's enemy and what he did about it. Tell me, convince me, and the money's yours. Looks like you could use it.'

His eyes went shrewd but I spoke again before he could say anything. 'You must've made good money in your job. Should've been able to live a bit better than this. Where did the money go?'

'Horses.'

'Don't you know the old song—horses don't bet on people and that's why they never go broke? Let's get down to it and don't bullshit me.'

'Have you got a tape-recorder on you?'

'No, this is between you and me and five hundred bucks.'

'Ronny told the kid's sister Ireland was fucking the mother.'

'I knew that.'

'The kid phoned Ireland and threatened to give the story to the media unless Ireland helped him.'

'How d'you know that?'

'Ireland got pissed and told me.'

'All right, I believe you so far. What did Justin want?'

'He wanted Wayne to arrange a false passport for him.'

'Wayne, eh? You were mates then?'

'We were, sort of, when it suited him. Not now.'

'How could Ireland do that? He's just a state government guy.'

'Fuck, you obviously don't know how it works. Those pricks've all got something on each other. Ireland could pull some Canberra strings when he had to. He's fuckin' pulling strings now, you'll see.'

'And?'

'He'll get seven years for manslaughter and serve five at the most. He's salted a fair bit away over and above his super, and they'll do a deal on that. He'll be okay.'

'Where does that leave you, Mike?'

'Fucked. They'll drop the perjury charge, I reckon, but I'll be out of a job and out of this billet. I've got diabetes and hepatitis, plus a gambling addiction. If you give me the five hundred I'll take it to Randwick and try to turn it into real money to get the fuck out of here. If I don't, I'm no worse off.'

It was a desperate scenario and he knew it. I had some sympathy for him, but not much. Not enough to let up.

'Did Ireland do what Justin wanted him to do?'

'I dunno. A lot of shit was hitting the fan in the political game just then and it never came up again when we were on the piss.'

'Why d'you think Ireland killed Angela Pettigrew?'

He shrugged. 'He's got an evil temper, especially when he's pissed. She was always threatening to expose him. She must've pushed a bit too hard.'

I thought about it, still holding the money. *If Ireland killed Angela because she threatened to expose him as an adulterer, what might he do to Justin, who had the same information and had tried to involve him in the sort of corruption that brought many a politician down?*

I dropped the notes on the blankets one by one. O'Connor's eyes followed their fall. My hand hovered over them.

'Ireland's probably gone to ground somewhere. D'you know where?'

'No.'

'He might have killed Justin Hampshire, too. What d'you reckon?'

O'Connor grabbed the notes with nicotine-stained fingers. 'I fuckin' hope so,' he said, 'and I hope you find out, you cunt.'

20

I was happy to get out of there and the information was certainly worth the five hundred. No sign of Ronny in the street. O'Connor would have to do without his cigarettes. These relationships I was running into—fathers and sons, mothers and daughters—made me glad I was childless. I stopped for a beer in a pub that was trying to look like a colonial inn and was doing a reasonable job of it. The beer was probably better, certainly colder.

I drove home with things on my mind, particularly the question of how to get to Wayne Ireland, so I was preoccupied when I pulled up outside my house, switched off the engine and took out the key. I only snapped out of it when I realised that a man was standing by my window with a gun in his hand. He made a winding motion and I lowered the window.

'Hands on the wheel, Hardy, and get out slowly. We're going on a little trip.'

The street was empty. Everybody was home and minding their own business. My neighbour on one side was away and the house on the other side was unoccupied, awaiting renovation. High hedges opposite.

I put my hands on the wheel but shook my head. 'I'm not in the mood.'

He leaned heavily on the wound-down window and pointed the pistol at my right knee. 'Sharkey wants to see you,' he said, 'and if your knee was buggered he wouldn't mind one little bit.'

What he didn't know was that the driver's side door on the Falcon didn't lock properly. I gripped the wheel and threw my weight against the door. It flew open and knocked him off-balance. I jumped out and chopped down hard on the arm carrying the pistol. It hurt me but it hurt him more. He dropped the pistol and I scooped it up as he came at me with a lowered head and fists flailing. I stepped aside, clipped him on the ear with the gun and let him cannon into the doorpost on the car. He went down and blood sprayed over the car, the road, his clothes and mine.

'Now look what you've done,' I said.

He was groaning and grabbing at his ear with one hand and his forehead with the other. The skin had split from the impact with the car, which added to the blood flow. Still holding the pistol, I kicked the door shut and he yelped as it closed a few inches from his head. He was game; he tried to get up but a fairly gentle push put him back down.

'You weren't quite up to it,' I said. 'Did Sharkey tell you it'd be easy?'

'Fuck you.'

A car that must have been parked further down the street with the engine running came slowly towards us. I let the driver see the gun.

'This'll be your mate,' I said. 'Not much use, was he?'

The car drew abreast of us and I gestured for the driver to get out and help his fallen comrade. He did it with very bad grace, getting blood on his trousers, swearing, fumbling. The injured guy abused him. I gave each of them a searching look while I held the gun in position. Standard hard types—bitter eyes and mouths, emotionally undernourished, mixtures of fear and hate.

'I'll know you both,' I said, 'don't come back.'

The car roared away with a squeal of tyres and whiff of burning rubber. I didn't know how long I'd been holding my breath, but I let it out now, slow and easy. I knew I'd been lucky, and luck was something you just couldn't rely on. I went to the end of the street, walked the block to the water and threw the pistol in. The last thing I needed was to have in my possession a gun that could've been used in shootings. I also didn't need the enmity of a heavy character like Sharkey Finn, but there was nothing I could do about that.

I went inside, filled a bucket with water and splashed it over the car to clean off the blood. I poured a solid scotch and sipped at it as I changed my pants and put the bloodied ones in the wash. I kicked off my shoes, which would need cleaning as well, and sat down with a second drink to think things over.

You didn't front up to a government minister, even one suspended and on bail, the way you did to his chauffeur. I didn't have any useful contacts in the political machine and Ireland was probably licking his wounds and conferring with his lawyers somewhere away from his usual haunts. O'Connor had said he didn't know where that might be. He'd wanted the money too much to risk a lie that I might trap him in. Ireland had a lot of problems and the only card I had to play was the information that he'd been involved in corruption by helping to provide a false passport—if he had. It wasn't an ace and I couldn't think of a way to play it. Hated to admit it, but I needed help. I rang Tania.

'Cliff, darling. I hope you've been busy.'

'I have. How's Sarah?'

'She's fine. Some news, I hope?'

There was no help for it, I had to tell her about Justin having seen Ireland and my need to talk to Ireland about it. It was risky—with Tania you never knew what use she might make of information. But this time she had her eye firmly on the game.

'That's good,' she said. 'Might give us a strong lead to Justin's whereabouts even after all this time.'

'Yes.'

I could almost see her chewing it over and, as I'd have predicted, she came up with the kind of strategy that was so dear to her heart: 'You could threaten to expose him as corrupt. He *has* to talk to you.'

'To use your expression, that's where you come in. You say you got to talk to him in the past even though it didn't go too well. I never heard that he was keen on the media. How did you manage it?'

You could always appeal to Tania's vanity. She allowed a dramatic pause before she spoke. 'I met Damien, his son, at a party and we had an affair. He's some kind of apparatchik in his father's office—sucking on the government tit. Damien set it up for me to get an interview with his father and that's why Wayne thought he could make me a father and son double. They'd done it before. Didn't quite get there, as I told you. They've got a weird relationship in that family. Damien idolises his dad *and* his mother. Is that a complex? Is there a name for it?'

'I don't know.'

'I think it's because they're Catholics with only one child. Sort of fixated on each other.'

'Still in touch with the son?'

'After the blow-out I had with his old man we're not exactly close, however he still had the hots for me last time I saw him. But I know something not too many people know.'

'Which is?'

'Where Wayne Ireland and son Damien go to do their rooting. I went there with Damien a time or two, and I'll bet that's where Wayne is right now.'

'Tell me.'

'No way. I'll show you.'

'Come on, Tania. It could get rough—the man's a drunk and probably desperate and he's killed one person already. And maybe another.'

'Who?'

'Perhaps the kid I'm hunting for. Anyway, you're supposed to be looking after Sarah.'

'We'll bring her along.'

'You're crazy. This isn't a film script you're writing.'

'Isn't it? Why not?'

I argued with her, threatened to turn the whole deal over to the police and to contact social services to say that she was an unfit person to be the carer of a vulnerable minor. She laughed at me.

'You've got it wrong, baby. She's turned sixteen. You know and I know the police'd never question Ireland on this matter the way he needs to be questioned. I mean pressured. You want the Justin enquiry to dead-end here? Sarah would thank you for that, I'm sure.'

She held the cards and she won the pot. The best chance for Sarah, financially and emotionally, was to resolve Justin's disappearance one way or the other. I went along with Tania's proposed arrangements with a few provisos of my own.

'No film crew along,' I said. 'Any sign of something like that and it's all off.'

'Okay. If we get to a movie we can always reconstruct. But I'm taping. No way I won't.'

That was reasonable and necessary. We haggled about a few details and eventually came to an agreement that made me unhappy. Still, it was the best I could do. I only scored one win—Sarah was to stay put. Tania fought it but, as everyone except Rocky Marciano found out, you can't win them all.

21

Tania insisted on driving her own car—a sporty 4WD Mitsubishi.

'That rust-bucket of yours'd never make it,' she said.

'So we're going up-country?'

'Wait and see.'

She'd left Sarah in the charge of a friend of hers who was also a lawyer. They'd talk over legal matters—plenty to sort out there.

'Fiona's very smart,' Tania said. 'She'll be a big help to Sarah and she can give her pointers on quite a few things.'

I didn't even want to know what that might mean. Tania wore her almost uniform of black pants and white blouse with a paisley scarf. The day had dawned cloudy with rain threatening, so she had a hooded parka. She also wore flat-heeled shoes, not her usual style, so I gathered there was some roughish ground to cover. Her leather bag carried various items, including a reporter's tape-recorder.

'With backup batteries,' she said when she showed it to me.

'And a camera, eh?'

'You never know what can pop up. I hope you've got your gun.'

'Wait and see. You reckon I could need it?'

'I told you, Ireland has some tough friends. Who knows who he's hanging out with now?'

I did have the .38, in a shoulder rig under my denim jacket. I had on drill trousers and boots so I was equipped for the country stuff. I'd never thought the Irelands would have their fuck-pad in the CBD.

Tania drove the way she behaved—recklessly, aggressively, with no consideration for others. She gunned the car through the traffic like a rally driver and had just enough experience and skill to avoid diaster. I hated to be a part of it and asked if we could have some music.

'No, I have to concentrate on my driving.'

'That's good; the way you drive, concentration is essential.'

'Fuck you.' She lit a cigarette and that was the end of conversation until her destination became clear.

'Blue Mountains?' I said.

'Got it in one.' She shot me a look, picking up a note in my tone. 'Something on your mind?' She broke into a fair Streisand imitation. '*Memories . . .*'

In fact I was thinking about Kathy's wish to see the Blue Mountains and my promise to take her. Going there now under these circumstances wasn't comfortable, felt like a small betrayal. I pushed the thought aside and tried to provoke Tania because I needed a distraction.

'Not really,' I said. 'How was Damien? Any good?'

She took a bend at speed and avoided an oncoming truck by too small a margin.

'Not the best, not the worst. What's the line in that crappy country and western song—"kinda dumb and kinda smart"? That's Damien. He had his points, liked certain . . . games. Interested in the details, Cliff?'

'Tania, your great talent is pissing people off. I doubt you'll ever win a Walkley. What's the minister likely to say when you front up?'

'He'll welcome me with open flies.'

'Why don't you just concentrate on your driving and getting us alive to wherever the fuck we're going.'

We left the Sydney plains behind and began the climb into the lower reaches of the Blue Mountains. The road should have been better than it was, given the traffic, and even Tania slowed down and took some care. The temperature dropped and a mist hung in the air, visible from a distance, not yet encroaching on the road.

I did have memories of times spent in the mountains, particularly a weekend with Cyn at the Hydro Majestic where the fog had rolled in and obscured the valley view that was billed as one of the great attractions of the place. It was very early on in our relationship and such things hadn't mattered much. We walked in the rain, sat by the fire, spent a lot of hours in bed. It was a long time back: a memory, not a wound.

We reached Wentworth Falls and Tania turned off onto a narrow road that quickly gave way to a roughly graded gravel stretch and then a dirt track where she engaged the four-wheel drive. The mist was thicker here and she had to flick the wipers on and off a few times to clear the windscreen. The track narrowed and trees overhung it. As we climbed the rain started and the wipers were needed full-time. She had to work to keep the car moving slowly, using the extra traction to avoid slides. She did it pretty well, but the strain showed in her face and she needed both hands. No smoking.

'Hernando's hideaway,' I said, just for something to say.

'They get a view of the lake on a good day, and some falls and other stuff. It was just a cabin until Ireland spent big money on it.'

'Jacuzzi? TV mast?'

'All that.'

'I hope he's here. It's a long way to come up empty.'

'He's here. I rang Damien last night.'

'Why doesn't that surprise me? Both of them here?'

'Who knows?'

'I suppose you gave him to understand he might have another crack.'

She smiled as she steered round a puddle. The front right-hand wheel went down into mud and only the extra drive power kept us going. We rounded a bend where the road widened out to allow for safety. The drop on the left looked like a plunge of a thousand feet into a misty void. A sign read 'Danger—Skinner's Leap' and a fence emphasised the fact. Then the track rose steeply for about half a mile before reaching a flat area of four or five acres. It snaked past, climbing higher.

Plenty of trees around the flat spot, some scrub, outcrops of rock. A cottage sat in the middle of the space—timber and glass, smoke drifting up from the chimney. There was no garden to speak of but an area beside the house had been cleared, levelled and closely mown. It had a flag on a six foot pole stuck in the middle of it.

'He's a keen golfer,' Tania said as she steered the car towards a cement slab where another car stood. 'Do you play, Cliff?'

'No. Strikes me the ball's too small and the distances are too big.'

'That's the fun of it. Well, here we go.'

She shrugged into her parka, pulled the hood up, opened the door and, tucking her bag under her arm, made a dash through the rain and mud to the front porch. I watched while she took off the parka and did something to her hair. She rang a bell. The door opened and she waltzed in. I zipped up my jacket, turned up the collar and got out. The rain was really just heavy drizzle and I tramped around to the other side of the house to check it out. A Land Rover, fire engine red, newish, gleaming in the pale light, stood under a tree. Wayne was not alone.

I continued my circuit and reached the back of the house, where a covered deck ran the full length. Tania was right about the view, even through mist and drizzle. Some trees had been dealt with to enhance it, and the result was a vista down towards the township with the lake in sight and the mist-clouded hills in the distance. I'm a citizen of the city and the beach, but this view brought me to a halt and I stood looking out over it, scarcely feeling the damp.

'Hey, Hardy. Come up out of the rain.'

I scraped my boots on the wire mat provided and climbed the steps to the deck, rubbing the water from my hair and unzipping my jacket. The man who met me was too young to be Wayne Ireland but had the same bull-like build I'd seen in photographs of the politician.

'Damien Ireland,' he said, holding out his hand.

I brushed my wet hands together. 'Got a towel?'

He didn't like my not shaking hands but he didn't want me to see it. 'Sure, Cliff,' he said. 'Come and I'll show you to the bathroom. Better wipe your feet again. Better still, take your boots off.'

I braced myself against the rail and removed my boots. Damien had a couple of inches over my six-foot-one and, as he was wearing boots too, he now had a big height advantage. Just for the hell of it, I took my socks off as well.

I went into a room that mirrored the deck, stretching across the whole length of the house—polished floors, rugs, a big fireplace, wood panelling, a bar with stools and a mirror. No hunting trophies. Tania and Wayne Ireland sat across from each other on either side of the fireplace. Both held drinks in one hand and were smoking—Tania a cigarette, Ireland a cigar.

'Cliff just has to dry off a bit, Dad,' Damien said.

Ireland senior nodded. 'Why don't you fix Cliff a drink.'

If they call me Cliff like that again, I thought, *we could have a serious problem.*

Ireland Junior pointed the way to the bathroom and I dried myself with a towel warm from a heated rail. When I got back he was standing behind the bar.

'What'll it be, Cliff?'

'Rough red.'

He was confused. 'Jesus, we haven't got—'

'I didn't think so.'

'Can't you see he's taking the piss?' Ireland Senior said. 'Pour him some red and let's get down to it here.'

I accepted a glass of red wine and went over to a chair between Ireland and Tania, a little back from them. Damien hovered in the background for a minute, then disappeared.

I seemed to remember reading that Wayne Ireland had played football. The frame that would have stood him in good stead then was overlain with fat. His face and neck were flabby and his expensive outdoor clothes didn't conceal a waistline bulge. He was 'hog fat' as the old bare-knuckle fighters used to say. His colour was high and the only healthy-looking thing about him was a crop of still dark, springy hair, growing thickly and worn long. It was carefully tended—about all he had left to be vain about, physically.

'Tania has put an interesting proposition to me, Hardy,' Ireland said. 'Very interesting.'

I sipped some of the very good wine and said nothing.

Tania flipped her cigarette into the fire and dug into her bag for the packet.

'Yes, she proposes that I give you certain information about an individual in whom you have an interest. In return she guarantees that the way in which I came by this information will remain confidential, and she will write several newspaper articles to help correct the bias against me that's currently being peddled.'

The pedantic phrasing and careful diction covered an underlying roughness, a legacy of a lower-class upbringing and schooling. Wayne Ireland had taken a long step vocally as well as in other ways.

'How do you know you can trust her?' I said. 'You know she'd sell her mother into white slavery to get what she wants.'

Tania sat up and almost spilled her drink. 'You bastard, you—'

'Keep your shirt on, love,' Ireland said, sounding more like the old unionist. 'He's just playing games with us, trying to assert himself.'

Tania delved for her lighter and lit up.

'Now, I find that proposition fairly attractive,' Ireland went on. 'As you know, I have certain legal problems. Not insurmountable, but I certainly don't need to add to them. I understand, Hardy, that you're in a position to do just that.'

'It could happen,' I said. 'Doesn't have to.'

'Exactly. I admire your dedication to your enquiry. Now, how should I put this? I was able to facilitate an individual . . .'

I could tell this wasn't going to work the way Tania had planned it. Where was Damien and what was he up to? And Ireland Senior was way too sure of himself for my liking. Time for some more self-assertion. I drained the wine glass and set it on the floor.

'Listen, Wayne, I don't give a fuck what names you mention or how you pussyfoot around the details. I only want to know two things—did you provide Justin Hampshire with a passport and, if so, in what name? That's it as far as I'm concerned. Tania can work out the subtleties with you however she likes.'

Ireland drew deeply on his cigar and tossed the long butt into the fire. 'Justin Arnold Pettigrew,' he said.

22

A bit stagily, Ireland opened a pigskin case, took out a cigar and lit it with a gas lighter. What he was drinking looked like whisky and he emptied his glass and let out a sigh. He looked tired, every day of his age and then some.

'I also gave him three thousand dollars.'

'That was . . . considerate,' Tania said.

'If it's true,' I said. 'How do I know you didn't solve your problem by killing him?'

'There's one very good reason why I wouldn't do that. He could've been my son.'

I was on my way to the bar but I stopped. 'What does that mean?'

'Why don't you get me some more scotch while you're at it? Angela said he was. She might've been telling the truth. We were rooting like rabbits at the relevant time. Mind you, Angela and Hampshire were cohabiting at that time, not so much later. The girl's certainly mine. She's the image of my sister when she was that young.'

'Ice or water?'

'Ice, thanks.'

I topped up my glass and made his drink in a fresh one. I handed it to him and he nodded. The events of the last week—the alleged killing of Angela Pettigrew and the political, social and economic fallout from the charge—had taken a severe toll of him. Some yellowing of his eyes and a sagging quality to his flabbiness suggested he wasn't eating and that his calories were coming mainly in liquid form.

'How could you just ignore them?' Tania said. She tossed her cigarette into the fire. 'Your own children.'

Ireland showed some of the spirit that must have made him a tough union organiser and a ruthless party and parliamentary operator. 'What would you know about it? What would you know about growing up in a housing department shithole with an alcoholic father and a mother on and off the game? I left school at fourteen barely able to read and write. It took me years to get enough confidence to write a fucking letter. I knocked my wife up at eighteen and it was hand-to-mouth for years.'

'That doesn't answer the question,' Tania said.

'Fuck you. I supported them. I propped up that stupid business of Angela's for years while her drongo of a husband went around conning people.'

He took a solid slug of his whisky and when he spoke next his voice was slurred. Like a lot of heavy drinkers, the dividing line between sober and drunk was a matter of millilitres.

'I'll tell you something off the fucking record. Some of the money I scammed went straight to Angela and her bloody kids.'

'That's enough, Dad.'

Damien had come in quietly. No way to tell how much he'd heard. He moved quickly and took the glass from his father's hand. Ireland sank back in his chair and stared into the fire as if he was seeing his past and future playing out in the flames.

Sometimes you have to kick a man when he's down. 'So you killed her,' I said.

Ireland nodded.

'No he didn't,' Damien said.

Ireland looked up, his blotchy face a mask of fear and confusion. 'Shut up, son.'

Damien was suddenly masterful and in control. He reached around to his back and produced a pistol. He held it in a rock-steady hand pointed directly at Tania's glossy head.

'No, Dad. You've made a big mistake. This bitch and her minder aren't here to do a deal. They're here to bleed you dry.'

'No!' Tania's normally modulated tone disintegrated.

I sat still. Damien had done exactly the right thing—focused the threat on the most vulnerable person. For all her raunchy facade, Tania had never faced a loaded firearm and it terrified her into an almost hypnotic state. Damien Ireland would be able to get her to do anything he wanted.

'Tania,' Damien said quietly, 'I want you to get up very slowly and put your sexy leather bag in my father's lap. Gently. I see it as two very slow movements.'

Tania did as she was told and almost collapsed back into her chair, still staring at the unwavering pistol.

'Reach in, Dad,' Damien said. 'London to a brick you'll find a tape-recorder running.'

Similarly mesmerised, Wayne Ireland did as his son instructed and produced the miniature tape-recorder. He held it to his ear and must have heard the faint tape hiss.

'You bitch,' he said. 'You were always going to fuck me over.'

'Chuck it in the fire, Dad.'

Ireland did. The recorder landed in the middle of the burning logs and erupted in a display of blue and yellow flames as the plastic caught and flared. Tania hid her face in her hands.

'I killed Angela Pettigrew,' Damien said.

'Jesus, son, no,' Ireland Senior said. 'It's just a manslaughter charge. The lawyers'll get me off. It's all circumstantial. Worst comes to worst I'll get a short sentence served somewhere soft.'

'I know that, Dad. We'll stick to the plan, but with your health the way it is that won't be a cakewalk and we can't trust this pair.'

Damien's control was frightening. Big and boofy as he was, and apparently under his father's thumb, I had underestimated him. Now I needed to unsettle him somehow. I took a sip of my drink.

'But you wouldn't get off it easily, Damien, would you? You'd go for murder, no worries. How and why did you do it?'

'She was blackmailing Dad and threatening to expose him as an adulterer and—'

'A corrupt thief,' I said.

'Shut your face. I followed him to the house and I finished her off after he left.'

'I see. Then you told him and persuaded him to take the rap.'

'No. He volunteered. That's the sort of father he is. He's giving up everything to protect me.'

Tania's terror had given way to wide-eyed fascination. Ireland Senior was shaking his head, muttering, pleading for his son to stop talking.

'That's bullshit,' I said. 'You're a mug if you believe that. This government's been on the skids since Nifty resigned. The two blokes after him have been hopeless. They're on the nose. You know as well as I do that Rex Jackson—the minister for prisons, for Christ's sake—is on the way to jail. Wayne here could easily be next. It's a corruption charge he's worried about. A conviction for that and they go after the assets. He's giving up less than he's protecting.'

'That's not true. Anyway, you're not going to be around to see how it plays out.'

Ireland shook his head. 'You can't kill them, son. There'll be people who know where they were going.'

'They never made it, Dad. They had an accident at Skinner's Leap. I've got a few mates coming up to help me with that.'

'No!' Wayne Ireland half rose from his chair and then sank back, gasping for breath and clutching his chest. He slid down and sideways and hit the floor, grunting and shaking.

'Dad!' Damien yelped. I was up and on him in three strides and laid the best tackle since my school days. He was so big he stayed on his feet but stumbled and I drove him back with my bare feet slipping on a rug but still getting traction. His back slammed into the bar hard and the gun fell from his hand. I scooped it up.

'Go and help him,' I said. I pulled out my gun in case his was a replica or unloaded—a bluff.

Damien lurched over to where Tania was trying to administer mouth to mouth resuscitation. Damien pushed her aside and took over. He was vigorous and seemed to know what he was doing. He was close to the fire and sweat poured off him as he pumped. He kept it up longer than I would have and was exhausted when he finally sat up.

'He's gone,' he moaned. 'Oh, God.'

He got to his feet, looked around wildly and began to cry. Tania tried to comfort him but he shoved her away and shambled out of the room.

Tania had had a couple of shocks too close together. Her face was white and she just managed to get back to her chair.

'Heart attack?' she said.

I nodded. 'He was holding a full hand for it.'

'You're a cold-blooded bastard, aren't you? Where's Damien?'

The roar of a motor answered the question. I went to the deck and saw the Land Rover ploughing through the mud, slewing and skidding as Damien gunned it harder than he should. I put my socks and boots back on and went inside. Tania had a cigarette going and she'd been to the bar for a stiffener. I poured myself some scotch and looked around the room. I straightened the rug that I'd buckled up. The tape-recorder had become a mass of molten plastic well on the way to being charred out of recognition. Ireland's cigar had landed on the brick hearth and was still burning. The only thing to suggest that Wayne Ireland hadn't simply suffered a heart attack when being interviewed was Damien's Beretta in my hand. It was loaded.

I went back to the deck and threw it as far into the bush as I could. I'd had a fair arm as a schoolboy cricketer and it disappeared deep into the misty greyness.

Tania joined me on the deck. 'What now?'

'We call an ambulance. This can't cause us any trouble. No suspicious circumstances.'

She was recovering fast but still wasn't quite there. 'What about Damien?'

'Nothing we can do there.'

It took an hour for the ambulance to arrive and the paramedics read it the only way they could. As they were placing Ireland on the stretcher one said, 'We were held up. A car went over the cliff at Skinner's Leap. Came from this direction.'

'Oh my God,' Tania said. 'Damien.'

The paramedic looked at her.

'Mr Ireland's son,' I said. 'He was very upset at the delay. He went for help, not that there was anything to do except just what you've done.'

'You'd better check in with the police at Katoomba about that, and we'll need your names and contact numbers and some ID.'

We showed them our drivers' licences, gave them the numbers and said we'd stop at the police station. They carried the heavy body from the house and loaded it into the ambulance. Dense rain was falling and the mist seemed to be rising up from the valley. We stood on the deck and watched the ambulance leave, the driver taking much more care than Damien had.

'Are there other houses further up the track?' I asked.

'Maybe one or two but they're weekenders. Wayne and Damien had their privacy. That had to be Damien who went over the edge. He was revving like crazy as he went. What are we going to do, Cliff?'

'Nothing. If they're both dead what does it matter who did what?'

'This didn't work out anything like the way we planned.'

'Could've been worse. Damien could have shot us both.'

'Oh, so you saved my life? Was he serious?'

I shrugged. 'The gun was loaded and he'd already killed one person.'

'Jesus, what about those friends Damien talked about?'

'With ambulances and police cars around, I don't think we'll be seeing them. Still, we'd better leave. Better to go to the cops than have them come to us.'

She gathered her bag and scarf. 'This is terrible.'

'Look on the bright side,' I said. 'You've got the scoop.'

23

The fence at Skinner's Leap was a tangled mess of wire and broken posts. We were waved down by the police stationed there and made a brief statement. We said we were going to report in at Katoomba and the office radioed that in.

'How far is the drop here?' I asked.

'Far enough,' the cop replied.

At Katoomba we gave a heavily edited version of what had happened at the Ireland house. The officers who took the statements didn't like the look of either of us, especially Tania, who was showing the effects of stress and alcohol. They kept going in and out of the room and conferring in private.

After we'd been there an hour the vehicle that had gone over the drop had been identified and was in the process of being recovered.

'You say he went for help,' one of the cops said, 'but the man was dead.'

I said, 'He'd busted a gut trying to resuscitate his father. The ambulance was a long time coming, he thought. He was upset and confused.'

'Drunk?'

'No. We—Ireland, Ms Kramer and me—had had a drink or two but he hadn't. Not that I saw. Tania?'

She shook her head. 'Can I smoke?'

The cop pushed an ashtray across the table. 'Sure.'

Tania fished in her bag and came up with an empty packet. The cop gave her one of his and she favoured him with one of her you're-the-only-person-in-the-world smiles. It was a bit lopsided and didn't work.

They got our details down in every last particular and let us go. Tania rushed to the nearest shop for cigarettes. I steered her to a coffee place and made her sit, eat a sandwich and drink a heavily sugared flat white.

'I have to admit,' she said, 'you handled that okay.'

'I've had the experience. We'd better get back so you can write your article.'

She was almost herself again now. 'Fuck that,' she said. 'I'm phoning it in to the copy-takers.'

Tania's story made a big splash in the afternoon edition and she strung it out over the next few days. Her articles were mostly factual with some speculation and some uncheckable lies. She didn't name me so I had no complaint. She'd cornered the market on the Ireland–Pettigrew story and I had to admit that she treated Justin's disappearance and Sarah's circumstances with discretion—no mention of paternity doubts. Damien's death was provisionally declared accidental and Tania presented herself as the last person to see him alive, leaving me out of it.

She speculated about whether Wayne or Damien Ireland had killed Angela Pettigrew, implying that her truncated interview with Wayne suggested he was the guilty party.

'Why did you go that way?' I asked her when we met up two days later.

'Kept the cops and the DPP happy and made for better copy. First state minister of the crown to commit a murder since the ex-minister Tom Ley in the forties. Similar in some ways, with mistresses and all that, but better, Wayne being in office at the time.'

In a sidebar to one of her articles she'd made a play of the Thomas Ley affair and his nefarious dealings, including a murder, after losing his ministry and parliamentary seat in New South Wales when in England in the 1940s.

'You don't miss a trick,' I said.

'A woman in this game? Can't afford to.'

That meeting took place after I'd had a talk with Sarah at Tania's house. Tania told me that the girl wanted to see me to ask about Justin. I told Sarah that Wayne Ireland had provided him with a passport and some money—something Tania had only hinted at—and that he must have left the country.

'Lucky bugger. That's what I'd like to do. Where did he go, Mr Hardy? To do what?'

'I think you know the answer to that question.'

'To be a soldier.'

'Yeah. I'll try to get the records searched, but he could've gone almost anywhere with a passport and some money. Lots of jumping-off points to other places. Lots of wars going on with opportunities for mercenaries—Lebanon, Angola, Nicaragua . . .'

'You think he got killed?'

'No way to tell. If he's alive and okay somewhere, eventually it's odds on he'll hear about what happened here. I never heard of an Australian overseas who didn't check back in some way, sooner or later.'

Sarah was smoking furiously and she lit another immediately after stubbing one out. 'If he hears about all this shit he probably wouldn't want to come back. He didn't care about me.'

'You don't know that. He was very distressed and not thinking clearly.'

She shook her head. 'I told you—we had a fight and I told him about Angela. I wish I hadn't.'

'Sarah—'

'Go away. Fuck off. I don't ever want to see you again.'

We were right back where we'd started and now I was sure she wasn't acting.

I was given a hard time by the coroner at the inquest on Paul Hampshire. Shouldn't you have taken steps to safeguard your client given the earlier events of the day? Shouldn't you have registered more details of the vehicle that struck him? Etc. Etc. The coroner was a soft-looking man in a tailored suit and my guess was that the only violence he'd ever have witnessed was from the sidelines in a Kings versus Shore rugby game.

Paul Hampshire's body was unclaimed for a time until some members of his old unit heard of his death and organised a service and a cremation. I went along out of a sense of responsibility, but not guilt. It was a sad affair for a man whose life had been pretty sad.

Things didn't improve. Tania didn't write her book but her articles got her a full-time job on one of the tabloids and her career prospered. On legal advice she withdrew her application to have Sarah put in her care and an aunt —a half-sister of Angela's—took over the job on the understanding that they would live in the Church Point house until the seven year period needed to declare Justin dead was up. By then, Sarah would be an adult and able to claim and dispose of her inheritance.

It didn't work out that way. Sarah and the aunt didn't get on and Sarah linked up again with Ronny O'Connor. They took as many valuable items from the house as they could manage, sold them, and used the proceeds to buy a motorbike. They went to Queensland and two years later they both OD'd in a Fortitude Valley squat.

About the time I got that news, from a friend in the PEA game in Brisbane, I met up again with Sharkey Finn. In a pub. But Sharkey had gone badly downhill from the grog and being dumped by Wilson Stafford, and when he challenged me his mate held him back and persuaded him not to be stupid.

The one bright spot was that Kathy Petersen came to Sydney at Easter. We went to the Blue Mountains and to the Central Coast and wined and dined and made love in a variety of places, including my house in Glebe, the Newport Arms hotel (where we joined in a celebration of the ALP's win in the federal election), and among the rocks at the south end of Maroubra beach. She went back to the coast and I visited her and it was still good, but she met another teacher and they transferred to a school further south and that was that.

Frank and Hilde got over the glitch I'd caused by roping her into my case. Peter got over Sarah, and by the age of fourteen he could beat Frank and me at pool and was pushing Frank at tennis. Taught by his mother, he became near-fluent in German and was studying Spanish and Italian.

Hans Van Der Harr's file on Justin disappeared. Tania said Sarah had taken it and probably destroyed it. That might have been right, but Tania was always economical with the truth. In any case, a few years later Van Der Harr was prosecuted for raping a female client while she was under hypnosis. He was deregistered and jailed.

There was no satisfaction to be had from the case and for a time I considered giving the game away, just for a while. No one had ended up happy except perhaps Tania. Was Damien a suicide or an accident victim? Sometimes it's like that—you don't know what's really going on until it's all over. And not even then.

My usual practice was to put all my notes and other documents on a case in a manilla folder and, when it was over, seal it with masking tape. Detective Sergeant Gunnarson at Missing Persons got onto the Immigration records and discovered that a Justin Pettigrew had left Australia for Singapore one week after Justin Hampshire's mother reported him missing, and there the trail ended. My case file on Justin Hampshire remained unsealed, open . . .

Epilogue

I rummaged in the box holding the bits and pieces I'd collected in the office, pulled out a roll of masking tape and sealed the file. I sat down and couldn't help thinking about Justin Hampshire, someone I never met but who had occupied a corner of my mind for years. I hated to think of him dead under a thorn bush in Africa or rotting away in some South American jungle, but that was the likely outcome.

I dropped the folder into the box with the others and took a last look around the room. I hadn't been there very long but it had grown on me. Hard to say how long Hank would be able to stay. This stretch of King Street was being tarted up quickly, and someone was bound to take over the shop below, spend money up here and raise the rent or need the space.

The wife, who'd prevailed upon Hank to give up PEA work in favour of installing security devices and providing computer upgrade services, had left him for greener pastures, and getting back to the kind of work he liked and did well was a good idea. I'd managed to transfer to Hank a couple of cases I'd been keeping warm while my licence cancellation was still under review. That would give him a start. Best I could do. I left the fax machine—hardly ever used these days—and the clunky old Mac laptop for his use. I suspected the Mac would find its way into the council clean-up service.

I locked the door and carried the boxes and a bag of garbage down to the car. Call me sentimental, but I'd arranged to have the Falcon put up on blocks in a friend's unused garage. He promised to start it up from time to time. I knew I'd be back, but I didn't know when, or what I'd be doing.

No time to think about that now. Frank and Hilde were waiting at Glebe to drive me to the airport. I had a plane to catch.